*Romances
by Jennifer Ashley*

LION
EYES

SHIFTERS
UNBOUND

JENNIFER
ASHLEY

Chapter One

Pain. Too much pain and too much blood.

Seamus heard snarling, vicious and deadly, felt his own throat sore. Had the sound come from him? Or whatever was attacking him in the dark?

Seamus fought like mad, the strength of his lion against whoever the hell it was. He thought he smelled Shifter, but in the dark and the madness of frenzy, scents were confused, whirling.

Seamus couldn't see, couldn't think. He clawed, bit, until his mouth was full of blood, his fur drenched with it.

He couldn't remember exactly where he'd been before this, only ducking and dodging through the fields, drawing whoever followed after him. He dimly remembered tucking those in his care safely into a house where no one would think to look, and then returning here to fool their enemies and lead them astray.

His life didn't matter. Those he protected did. Seamus was a tracker, a soldier with a job to do.

Except that his brain kept blanking out, fighting instincts taking over and making everything a blur.

Feral. The word whispered through his brain — the fear every Shifter had, especially those who'd never taken the Collar.

Seamus had been feeling it for a few weeks now, ever since the bunker had been taken over and the Shifters within forced to scatter. His assignment, protecting those put in his charge from the wide, bad world and everyone in it. The task had heightened his wariness, shooting high the nagging feeling that *something* was just on the edge of his vision, waiting.

Edgy, paranoid, easily provoked into fighting, Seamus had moved his charges from one safe house to another.

Now his raw animal instincts had taken over. Maybe *this* was what going feral was like. No thinking, just reacting, wanting to fight, hurt, *kill.*

Seamus struck and struck again. He smelled blood, heard desperate male screams. And then, whatever battled him ... vanished.

Seamus forced his way back, second by second, to sanity.

Cool November wind rippled his lion's mane, bringing the scent of dust and weeds, and the faint smell of exhaust from the trucks and motorcycles around the roadhouse in the distance. Music drifted from the building, and the sound of Shifters, the kind with Collars.

He changed. Seamus's bones ached as they shrank and moved, sinews twisting and readjusting around the new form. His sight went from a concave, wide view that picked up all shadows, to a narrow focus that didn't see as well in the dark. He straightened his back, hearing vertebrae pop, and turned around.

Two men lay dead at his feet. Human, not Shifter. A Shifter had ripped them apart—the brute strength that had pulled them inside out could only have come from someone like Seamus. Pieces of the hunters' broken shotguns were scattered about the dried Texas grass.

Seamus's breath clogged his throat. The scent of death and blood was horrific, blotting out all thought.

He'd believed he'd smelled Shifter as he'd fought, but the only Shifter within sight, hearing, and scent, was himself.

Seamus, un-Collared, on the run, fearing that the craziness he'd been feeling in these last weeks was the beginning of the feral state, was standing over a couple of dead bodies.

His clothes—T-shirt, jeans, boots—lay in a simple pile a few yards away. Barely able to breathe, Seamus quickly pulled them on as he pondered what he should do.

"There!" someone shouted in the darkness of the fields. "Get him!"

Shite. Seamus figured he knew exactly who the human voices were yelling about. He turned and ran.

A shotgun boomed at the same time he heard the retort of a rifle firing then firing again. Pain blossomed in his side, but Seamus kept running. He headed to the edge of the roadhouse parking lot, knowing he'd have to steal a vehicle to get away.

Kendrick, his leader, would shit a brick, but then, life sucked for an un-Collared Shifter on the run.

***

Bree Fayette vowed to give up the life of a Shifter groupie. That was it—over—she was done.

She decided this as she looked into the eyes of three fanatical women outside the back door of the roadhouse, where they'd dragged her. Two had their faces painted with the usual Feline makeup; one wore Lupine ears and a T-shirt with a wolf on it.

"This is *our* place," the wolf woman said. "Time to go, honey."

Bree had come here tonight to meet people who shared her interest in Shifters, but she'd decided, as soon as she'd walked into the roadhouse between Austin and San Antonio, that she'd made a mistake.

She'd had time to order one drink, which she hadn't even finished, for crying out loud, before the other women converged on her. The Shifters, who seemed a bit wilder than the ones she'd encountered in New Orleans, hadn't come to her aid. They didn't know her, and Shifters avoided humans they hadn't vetted.

Before Bree could decide that retreat was the better part of valor, the groupie women had taken her by the arms and forcibly dragged her out the back door. She fought, but lost.

"Is this how you greet new people around here?" Bree asked the women as she tried to catch her breath. "Real hospitable of you. I'm so glad I ventured out tonight."

"Just take a hike," one of the women with cat's ears said. "These are *our* Shifters. We take care of them."

Meaning they were very protective. Of course — Bree might be a spy for the police, reporting on which Shifters were breaking the many rules they had to follow.

"I'm not a threat," Bree said in a hard voice. "I'd never do anything to hurt them."

The three women weren't convinced. "You come here with a Shifter of your own, and maybe we'll believe you," the wolf woman said. "For now, get out while you can."

Bree heaved a sigh. She'd never win a full-blown fight against these three and knew it. She decided to leave while she still had some dignity. "Fine. I'm going."

She had to push past them. The women folded their arms, expressions unyielding as Bree bumped by them and headed to the end of the lot where she'd parked her truck. She felt their gazes on her all the way, then she heard the thump of the back door slamming. She looked back to find the women gone, the door closed, shutting her out.

So ... *that* had gone well. These Texas women were crazy bitches. Not like the fun-loving Shifter-stalkers that were her New Orleans friends. Bree and her girlfriends weren't Shifter whores or anything — they just liked to *look* at the tall, gorgeous alpha guys who could turn into animals. They wanted to talk to them, hang out with them, be around them. One of Bree's friends even kept a website about Shifters and a much-read blog.

Bree and her mom had moved out here from Louisiana this winter, but between Bree making sure her mother was settling in, not to mention both of them coping with Remy's death, she hadn't had a chance to get to know many people. She'd thought she could come here tonight and meet ladies, and guys, who shared her interest in Shifters, but apparently, she'd been wrong.

Her loneliness rose up on her wave of anger, and she blinked back tears. *Damn, I miss you, Remy.*

Bree's cell phone rang as she climbed into the black F250 pickup that had belonged to her brother — *God rest his soul and keep him safe.* She knew that ringtone. *Figures.*

Bree answered as she settled into the driver's seat. "Hello, Mom." She sagged back and studied herself in the rearview, dusty light reflecting from the parking lot. "Yes, I'm fine." A slight exaggeration. Her makeup was smeared, one of her fake cat's ears torn, and her tail had been pulled off, lost somewhere in the darkness of the bar. "Yes, I'll remember to stop and pick up your smokes. No, I didn't make any new friends, not yet." Another pause while her mother really got going. Bree started the pickup. "No, Mom, I'm *fine.* I swear to you, it's a perfectly normal Shifter bar." For one with a bunch of maniacal groupies and crazy Shifters in it. "No meth heads, no drugs at all. It's a nice, quiet little place ... Really quiet and nice —"

Something hit Bree's pickup full force.

Bree whipped her head around as a man landed in the pickup's bed and swarmed up to the cab. She watched in numb astonishment as he swung his long body feet-first into the cab through the open passenger window.

"Bree? Are you still there?" came the strident tones of her mother. "If you've hung up on me ..."

The man landed on the seat, closed a huge hand around Bree's cell phone, and threw the phone out the open window.

Bree's frozen moment of amazement broke. She clung to the steering wheel, opened her mouth, and screamed as loudly as she could.

The man was across the seat in a heartbeat, clapping a strong and dirt-streaked hand over her mouth. "Drive," he said, his voice so guttural she could barely understand the word. "*Now!*"

No way in hell was Bree going anywhere with this guy. She'd fight him off, run back inside the bar, yell for help. Who cared that the groupies were unfriendly? She'd hide out in the bathroom and let the bouncers deal with him.

Two more men materialized out of the dark. They had shotguns, and they pointed them at the man and at Bree.

"*Go!*" the man roared.

The shotguns boomed. Bree's truck wasn't there to receive the blast, though, because she'd stomped on the gas.

The pickup jumped forward and hit the ground, wheels spinning. A thick cloud of dust boiled up behind them as Bree shot out of the parking lot to the road.

The road itself was dirt, washboard rough, slippery with dust that weeks without rain had made bone dry. Another shot rang out behind them, and Bree's right mirror shattered.

She screamed again and pushed harder on the gas. The truck shimmied and danced, but Bree had helped Remy rebuild this baby, and she knew it inside and out. She expertly maneuvered up and down the washes and out to a paved road.

Bree raced down this empty stretch of back highway for a minute or so, until multiple glances behind them told her no one was following. Not yet, anyway.

She swung to the grass at the side and slammed the truck to a halt. "Get out," she said firmly.

The man who looked back at her in the dark didn't move. He was a Shifter—she'd guessed that the moment he'd leapt with the grace of an acrobat into the cab. His large body took up most of the passenger seat, dark T-shirt stretching over a tight chest and arms that could lift this pickup if he wanted to. His hair was cut short but a mess, black, she thought, though it was hard to tell in this light.

His eyes ... They were golden, intense, pinning her as Bree stared at him in shock. *Lion eyes,* whispered through her head.

The Shifter wildcats—Fae cats, they called themselves—had been bred to mix the best qualities of big cats, but individual Feline clans tended to favor one species or other. Leopards, jaguars, cheetahs, and mountain lions were most common.

Tigers were very, very rare—so rare Bree knew about only one of them.

And then there were the lions. The Morrissey family, who ran the Austin Shiftertown, were black-maned lions. She'd seen photos of the men of that pride on the Internet, but she'd never seen this Shifter.

He cranked around in his seat to look behind them. "It's not safe to stop here," he said in an accent that sounded faintly ... Scottish? Irish? Bree was no expert on accents other than those around her hometown. "Keep going."

Bree didn't answer. She was staring at his neck, more of it revealed when he'd turned his head.

He wasn't wearing a Collar.

All Shifters wore Collars. It was the law. Collars had some kind of chip in them that triggered a series of nasty shocks when the Shifter who wore it became violent. There were those who claimed that the Collars also contained Fae magic, meant to control the Shifters, though Bree was a little skeptical about the magic part. But then, shape-shifters had turned out to be real, so who knew?

This Shifter had no chain of silver-and-black links around his neck, no Celtic knot at his throat. No red line around his neck to show that he'd pulled his off either—the Collars were embedded into the skin for life.

Bree was terrified at the same time her insatiable curiosity rose and demanded to be satisfied. It would get her killed one day, that curiosity, her mother always said. Well, maybe today was the day.

"Are you feral?" she asked cautiously.

Feral Shifters were those who had left any civilized behavior behind and were becoming wild animals, nothing more, no matter what their shape. Bree had heard they usually stopped bathing and wearing clothes, and this guy was definitely dressed—jeans, T-shirt, and motorcycle boots. Though she saw black smears on his skin, he didn't look like he'd missed many showers.

He stared at her with those golden, lion eyes, and said, "Maybe. Not yet. Now, *go*."

"Or, *I* can go, and you can *get the hell out of my truck*."

"Damn you," he said, his voice quietly desperate. "I'm dead the minute I hit the ground."

Bree's heart pounded sickeningly, but she remained in place. "You weren't at the bar. Are you from one of the Shiftertowns around here?"

He was over the seat and right next to Bree before she could blink. His foot slid alongside hers and pushed the gas.

The truck leapt. Bree grabbed the steering wheel, cranking it around before they slid into the ditch. The pickup hit the pavement, shimmying until Bree righted it and sent them down the road in the correct lane.

At least the Shifter had moved his foot once she'd got the truck going.

"I don't care where you take me," he said. "Just get me away from the hunters."

Bree peered down the dark road, a straight stretch, empty this late. They were a long way from Austin, a long way from anywhere, really.

Lights appeared behind her. The hunters? Hard to tell, but the lights were coming up too fast. The Shifter next to her twisted in the seat to look back at them. "Hell — *go!*"

The headlights got larger, far quicker than they should have. Bree's breath came too fast, her blood pumping. She'd been chased before. She hadn't liked it then, and she didn't like it now.

"All right, all right." Bree shoved her foot down on the gas, the truck rushing forward. The speedometer crept past sixty, seventy, eighty.

"Who are you?" she repeated over the engine's noise. "What Shifter clan are you with, and why aren't you wearing a Collar?"

The man said nothing. Bree risked turning her head to find herself pinned by his golden stare.

"Why do you know so much about Shifters?" he demanded.

Bree waved her hand at her made-up face as she focused on the road again. Her eyeliner had started to run, forming black tears. "Hello? I'm a Shifter groupie. We know *everything* about Shifters. The clans, the prides and packs, the family trees. What you can do and can't do, where you live, who your mates are, what the Collars do. I'm not as into it as some of my friends back home — they would know *exactly* who you were and where you came from. Kind of creepy, right?"

He kept scrutinizing her, like a big cat trying to decide whether or not to pounce on a gazelle. "My name's Seamus."

"Nice Irish name. You Irish?"

"No."

He snarled it. Bree let out her breath. "All right. No need to bite my head off."

More scrutinizing. Maybe she shouldn't have mentioned biting—he was the most predatory Shifter she'd ever met. Probably because he didn't have a Collar. *Why* didn't he? What …

The black truck in her rearview put on a sudden burst of speed. The crazy driver shoved the truck between Bree and the right-hand side of the road, on the very narrow shoulder. One wrong bump, and they'd both flip.

Apparently, the driver didn't care. Three guys in the bed of the other truck had shotguns, and they lifted them and pointed them at Bree and Seamus.

"Shit!" Bree yelled. Her instinct was to slam on the brakes and let the other truck shoot forward, but the truck might hit her, and they'd all be whirling across the road to likely death.

"Pull over and give us the Shifter!" the driver called through his open window.

"No way in hell!" Bree shouted back. Only one thing to do. "Hold on," she told Seamus.

Seamus must have seen something in her expression, because he stopped snarling and closed his hands around the seat.

What the hunters didn't know was that this truck had belonged to Remy Fayette, Bree's brother, before his military stint in the Middle East had ended his life. A missile had taken out the helicopter he and his team had been in, while carrying out a rescue mission. The army had given Remy a hero's burial, and their mom a flag and a little money in the bank every month. Bree kept the truck in his memory.

Before Remy had given up his wild life for the discipline of the army, he'd spent his time modifying cars and trucks and racing them—legally and not so legally. Bree sent him a silent blessing as she flipped a switch to deploy the nitrous oxide boost.

The pickup shot forward, jerking Bree and the Shifter. The truck following them dropped instantly behind. Ninety miles an hour, a hundred. Bree hung on to the steering wheel for dear life.

The headlights behind them swiftly grew smaller. Seamus was clutching the seat so hard his fingers tore the upholstery.

"Whoo—hoo!!" Bree yelled. "Eat that, dirtbags! Thank you, Remy Fayette. I love you!"

As usual, when Bree thought of her brother, her eyes filled with instant tears. *Not now.* She had to drive, to see the road.

She also had to get them to ground somewhere. Bree couldn't keep this speed without attracting every highway patrol in the county, but if she slowed down, the guys chasing Seamus might find them.

Nothing for it.

"I'll take you to a Shiftertown," she said. "Which one are you from?"

Seamus's gaze was on her again, unrelenting. "*No.* No Shiftertowns. Just put enough distance between us and them." He had a hand on the door handle, as though contemplating when it would be safe to jump out. *What the hell?*

Something bad was going on here. At the same time, Seamus was a Shifter, and those guys chasing him were ready to shoot him. He'd be safe in a Shiftertown, where hunters didn't dare go—they weren't allowed to bother Collared Shifters. But if Seamus refused to go to a Shiftertown, then where?

"I have an idea," Bree said. "I know a place you can lie low. Not the best choice, but no one will think of looking for you there."

Seamus didn't answer. He glanced behind them again, and his body finally relaxed. The headlights were gone.

Bree turned off the extra juice. The truck slowed abruptly, rattling and bumping. Remy had taught her how to drive a rod though, and Bree maneuvered the truck to handle the sudden change in speed. She took the next corner, heading off into the darkness of the back roads.

"Where?" Seamus asked, his voice harsh.

"You'll see," Bree answered. "I'm just telling you now, though—*you* get to explain why you threw away my cell phone while I was talking to my mom."

Chapter Two

The young woman took Seamus to a house comfortably far away from any Shiftertown. Seamus wasn't sure exactly where he was, but he could sense that no Shifters were nearby, nor had they ever been there.

The horizon showed a smudge of light — reflected light of a city — but the half-mile drive the young woman with smeared makeup turned up was bathed in darkness.

That is until she pulled the truck to a stop. Instantly, flood lights burst on to surround the truck, the young woman, a white painted house, and a white-fenced flower garden in harsh yellow light.

The screen door of the house's porch banged open and a woman cradling a slim shotgun emerged. "Who's there?"

"It's me," the younger woman said in irritation as she slid from the pickup's cab. "Who do you think, in this truck? Put that away before you hurt yourself."

The shotgun's barrel moved to Seamus. "Who's he?"

"A Shifter," the young woman continued as she approached the house. "This is Seamus. He needs a place to crash. Geez, Mom, would you turn off the lights? It's like Las Vegas out here."

The woman on the porch had short, very blond hair that stuck up in points, and wore a colorful, flowing garment that reached her feet. She competently held the gun, the eyes over it a hard blue. A woman who'd seen tough times. Her daughter's short, curly hair was a golden wheat color, so it was likely the mother's blond was not natural. Mother and daughter shared the same eyes, but the daughter's look was sad rather than hard.

The younger woman was nicely shaped, with curves outlined by her short leather skirt and a white top that bared plump shoulders and a modest amount of cleavage. The young woman carried a cat's ears headband and had painted slanted points to her eyes and whiskers around her nose and mouth.

Shifter groupies liked to dress like this, so Seamus had heard, though he'd not encountered groupies much before tonight. Kendrick's Shifters had to be careful what bars they went to, and Seamus had always been too busy with tracker duties to go out much.

The young woman walked confidently up to the porch, took the shotgun out of the older woman's hands, and uncocked it.

"Come on in, Seamus," she called back to him, her eyes meeting his in a sweep of blue. "My name's Bree, by the way, and this is my mom. You can call her Nadine, or you can call her Mom. Whichever is most comfortable for you."

Bree's mother scowled. "None of your lip, Bree. You should have told me you were bringing home a guest. I would have fixed something."

Bree ignored her to wave Seamus to follow. "No one chasing you with guns here. At least, not anymore." She disappeared inside through the screened porch.

Seamus hesitated. He didn't believe that Bree or her mother were a danger, at least none that he could immediately perceive. But he could bring *them* danger. More than they understood.

Nadine called after her daughter. "Why did you hang up on me out there? I was talking to you."

"Ask *him*," Bree said from somewhere inside the house.

Nadine snapped around to Seamus and gave him an impatient look. "Are you coming in, or what? If I leave this door open any longer, every bug in Texas will get inside. And damn, they have a lot of bugs out here."

"Like they don't in Louisiana?" Bree's voice floated out. She said the state's name with all the vowels slurred, like *Looziana*.

Nadine reached one hand inside the house. The lights died, leaving only a small glow over the door.

Seamus's tension eased—he preferred to be in darkness as the observer, not lit up and observed. He made his decision, quickly skimmed up the porch stairs past Nadine, and entered the house.

Nadine banged the screen door shut. "'Bout time you made up your mind. Bree, did you pick up my cigarettes?"

A sound of annoyance and running water came from behind a door under a flight of stairs. "No, I did not get your cigarettes. I was *busy!*"

"Busy chasing Shifters?" Nadine looked Seamus up and down, her hands on her hips. "I see you caught one. Bree, you are not having sex with him in your bedroom. You hear me?" Nadine broke off. "What's he doing?"

Seamus was moving through the house, checking everything. A painfully neat living room ran from front door to back, an alcove with a dining table lay behind the staircase, and a door in the dining area's wall opened to a very large kitchen.

Another door in the kitchen led to the back yard. Seamus crossed the kitchen and opened the door to find all quiet outside, except for a striped cat who came pattering up the back porch's two steps to Seamus as soon as he emerged.

The cat followed him inside, twining around his legs as he walked through the kitchen to the living room again. Cats liked Feline Shifters, and Seamus in particular.

Seamus walked past Nadine and started up the stairs as Bree emerged from the ground-floor bathroom, wiping her dripping face.

Nadine called after Seamus. "What did I just say? No Shifters in the bedrooms."

"Leave him alone," Bree said. "He's walking his bounds."

Seamus allowed himself to feel a touch of amusement. He was angry, scared shitless, and in pain, but this girl, Bree, was ... interesting.

There was more to her than met the eye, that was certain. When he'd jumped into her truck, Bree had been terrified, but she'd quickly rallied into anger and then resourcefulness. She'd understood the danger the Shifter hunters posed, and she could think on her feet.

Upstairs Seamus found two bedrooms and a bathroom, each as neat as the rooms downstairs. The furniture was comfortable, not showy, but clean and tidy, the hardwood floors polished.

A square of ceiling on the landing likely led to an attic above. Seamus was tall enough to reach up and push the square aside to reveal a dark hole. No ladder was in sight, so Seamus leapt, caught the edges of the opening, and hoisted himself up and inside. The cat sat down on the landing and meowed.

The attic, unlike the rest of the house was dusty, dark, unused. Seamus could see well enough in the dim light, even without shifting to his wildcat, to discover what was up there.

Not much. Boxes smelling musty, pipes for the rest of the house, debris that looked as though it had been left over from the house's last remodeling.

Seamus didn't like the slightly acrid smell, so different from the clean house downstairs. He wondered why the two women hadn't come up here and thrown away all this junk.

No men were in the house. Bree and her mother lived alone, and one of them smoked — a lot. Seamus wondered why humans loved inhaling toxic chemicals. He could see the bands of poison sliding into them and not coming out.

He slid back down through the hole, landing on his booted feet. Bree and her mother had joined the cat, three stares on Seamus as he straightened up and dusted off his hands on his jeans.

Bree's eyes, now free of groupie makeup, were undisguised, soft, and blue. She looked him over, taking in the streaks of dirt on his arms, which hid the now-dried blood, his hair, which must be a mess, his face that had to be as filthy as the rest of him. His clothes kept her from seeing how hurt he was, which he would shut up about until he decided what to do.

Bree moved her scrutiny from him to the attic. "What's up there? I haven't had the chance to look."

"Old stuff," Seamus said. "You should have a clear out."

"Ghosts," Nadine put in decidedly. She had a cigarette in her mouth, a lighter clicking. "The place is haunted. You can hear them banging around up there at night. This house belonged to my uncle. When he died, we got a nice yard, a paid-for house, and ghosts."

Bree rolled her eyes. "It's not haunted. Birds get in through the vents."

"Well, there's *something* up there. What did you see, Shifter?"

"No ghosts," Seamus said. "Not at the moment. We're alone."

Bree and her mother exchanged a glance. They were uncomfortable, uncertain of him, though not completely afraid.

Whoever he'd been fighting in the dark tonight had been so afraid of Seamus the terror had rolled over him in waves. Rage had flowed over him as well—or had that been his own? The fear as well? The remembered feel of terror and anger started to bring his darkness back, the lack of air, the blurring of his brain.

Seamus was suddenly exhausted, the pain making him weak. He needed to sleep, to heal—he didn't know if he could trust these two to guard him when he did. Or even if they could.

Nadine took over. "Well, we are marching back downstairs. And you, young man, are going to tell us why you made Bree bring you here."

"He didn't …" Bree flipped her hands in a gesture of surrender. "Never mind. I need coffee. And I want to hear why those guys were chasing you too. Downstairs. Go."

Seamus did not obey, but Bree brushed past him, filling him with a scent like violets. He turned his head to watch her go down, noticing the way her hips swayed under the leather skirt.

When he turned back, he found Nadine right under his nose. She blew out cigarette smoke, making his eyes screw up. Seamus held back a cough.

"I have my eye on you," Nadine said severely. "You go easy on my girl. She's grieving. If you hurt her in any way, I'll shoot you through the heart."

"Mom!" The exasperated word came up the stairs. "Leave him alone."

The end of the cigarette glowed as Nadine took another pull. "You understand me?"

Seamus was too fatigued to argue, so he gave her a nod, turned away, and went downstairs after Bree. Nadine followed him. Closely. Her cloud of smoke engulfed him.

Seamus checked the ground floor again as Bree clanked things in the kitchen. The shotgun was nowhere in sight — Bree must have secured it. She'd known how to carry it safely, respectfully. Seamus hated guns, as most Shifters did, and he was glad that at least Bree wasn't careless with it.

The front door was the most defensible — an intruder would have to navigate the porch's screen door, the porch itself, and the main door in order to enter. Plenty of time for Seamus to hear them coming, to get the females to safety, to counterattack.

The floodlights had a motion sensor, Seamus discovered when he and the cat walked outside to check the truck and scan the grounds. Anyone approaching would be instantly seen.

All was quiet. A line of houses began to the west about a mile away, separated from this house by an empty field. The other three directions also held empty fields — one had what looked like a large, upright sign in the middle. Trees densely lined the far side of the field to the north, showing the presence of water, most likely a creek, one of the myriad of waterways in this area.

Seamus walked around the house to the back, wondering what the hell to do. He needed to make sure his people were safe, but he couldn't risk leading anyone to them right now. He was too weak to fight, would be too slow to get them to another place. And he was running out of safe houses. At some point tonight, he'd simply fall over, and he needed to secure himself before then.

Who to trust? Could he trust *anyone* while waiting for Kendrick's signal? He couldn't risk revealing the wrong information to the wrong people.

The name Dylan Morrissey was talked about, but Dylan was a Collared Shifter, high in power. The Morrisseys captured rogue Shifters, he'd heard, brought them in, put Collars on them, tried to tame them if they were feral. Killed them if they couldn't be tamed. No, the Morrisseys were not an option, especially when Seamus feared he might be going feral himself.

If he could get word to Kendrick … Seamus was one of Kendrick's trackers—a fighter, guard, scout, and spy.

He had responsibilities, protocol to follow now that they'd had to go to ground. Keep his head down, protect those he was assigned to protect, stay sane and free, regroup. Standing procedure.

At all other times, standing procedure worked well. This time…

Seamus swallowed another grunt of pain and let himself in the kitchen door. This entrance was the most vulnerable, with no screen and only a small porch with steps leading to it. If he battered the stairs away, he decided, an enemy would have to jump or climb to get to the door, giving Seamus some advantage.

Bree and Nadine looked up from where Bree was setting coffee on the table. So many windows in this room, in the entire house. Too many places a shot could come through and injure those within. Bunkers were much safer.

Not that the bunker Seamus had been living in until recently hadn't been breached by a Kodiak she-bear, a human soldier, and a crazy wolf Shifter. Hence, Seamus was on the run, cut off from his clan and leader, trying to guard those in his care and not go insane at the same time.

The coffee smelled good. The beverage was a human affectation Seamus had taken up with pleasure. He dropped into a chair, grabbed the cup, and poured the steaming brew down his throat.

Bree and Nadine watched him in alarm. Nadine was stubbing out her cigarette, the smoke thankfully dissipating.

Bree sat down across the table from Seamus and lifted her cup to her lips. Blue eyes flecked with green regarded him with interest. Seamus watched Bree's red mouth touch the coffee cup, narrow to a pucker as she sipped, and then her tongue come out as she licked away a lingering drop.

Despite his pain, Seamus went tight. It had been a long time, this woman had rescued him, whether she'd meant to or not, and his progressing madness heightened all frenzy — mating as well as killing.

The pain wasn't dampening his sudden need either. Seamus drained his cup, thumped it back to the table, and couldn't stop a sound of discomfort. He needed to crawl away and sleep, heal.

"Are you hurt?" Bree was up and at his side, her eyes filled with concern.

"I'm Shifter," Seamus said through his teeth. "I mend fast."

"Let me see." Bree's top slid, letting him glimpse a pillow of breast as she bent over him. Wisps of her short hair brushed his cheek as her hand went unerringly to the place Seamus hurt most.

He couldn't stop his gasp. Fighters and trackers couldn't show weakness, even to the females of the pack. They had one job to do, and they'd go down doing it.

Bree managed to peel Seamus's black shirt up to expose the dried blood and bruising on his ribs. "Shit," she exclaimed, her eyes widening. "You didn't mention you'd been *shot.*"

Chapter Three

Bree's fingers went cold as she studied the small holes in Seamus's skin, the blackened blood, the purple-black of the bruises. The way he'd moved getting into her truck, the way he'd wandered restlessly in and around her house had betrayed no pain or discomfort. Not until Seamus had started to relax had he showed any hurt.

Seamus's hand curled to a fist as Bree pried the shirt away, but other than that, he breathed without a hitch, and the rest of his skin was smooth and whole, if a little pale from the wound.

The abs the shirt had clung to were hard and well-formed, an arrow of dark hair pointing to his belt buckle. He was a big man, as most Shifter males were, but he was more lithe, like a gymnast or acrobat. Old scars and one mottled chunk of skin gone from his right side in a long-ago injury told Bree he was a fighter. A soldier, like Remy.

A soldier who'd definitely taken a bullet tonight, or two, or three.

Bree's mom was up, cigarettes abandoned. She bent over Seamus, gave the wound a glance, and rushed out of the kitchen, her muumuu fluttering.

"How long ago?" Bree asked.

Seamus was regarding her in quiet surprise. He'd probably thought she'd turn green and pass out at the sight of his blood. "Right before I found you and your truck."

It was Bree's turn to be surprised. "Seriously? This looks days old — but wait, you're Shifter. You heal differently than we do."

"Faster," Seamus said. "Not much different. Healing is healing." He winced. "It still fucking hurts."

"I bet." Bree touched his skin as close to the wound as she dared. "Mom's getting her fix-up kit. We'll get you taken care of."

She heard Nadine clatter down the stairs, and in a moment, her mother was back, setting the big tackle box that was their first-aid kit on the table.

"How many bullets?" Nadine asked Seamus.

"Three." Seamus's voice was getting weaker. "And a few scatters of shot."

He looked pretty good for someone who'd taken three bullets and some pellet. Bree kept stroking his side below the wound, liking the warm, taut feel of his skin.

"Get your shirt all the way off," Nadine ordered.

Seamus obeyed without question, his supple arms moving quickly as he bunched the shirt in his hands and pulled it over his head. A man used to being given commands, but knowing which commands were wise to follow. A soldier, as Bree had surmised.

Seamus balled the shirt, as though he didn't want to drop it on the floor. "I don't have anything to knock you out with," Nadine was saying. "Unless you want to get roaring drunk."

"No," Seamus said tightly.

Nadine laid out tweezers, alcohol, a scalpel, and bandages. "Bree and I are going to take out the bullets. Shifters might heal fast, but you can't do it with slugs lodged in you. You're lucky they're shallow, just by the ribs. Don't worry, I was a nurse way back when, and I've taught Bree everything I know. Came in handy, living out in the middle of nowhere like we used to. My son managed to get himself peppered with shot more than once in his wilder days, and medical help was hours away. Easier to patch him up and then drive him to the hospital."

Remy had sure yelled, Bree remembered with a rush of fondness, but conceded it was his own stupid fault — he'd trespass on lands of crazy people or walk in front of a hunter notorious for shooting anything that moved.

Tears moistened Bree's eyes. Remy had been good at dodging and ducking, managing to avoid the worst of it. But he hadn't been able to dodge when the missile had come for the helicopter, exploding it in the middle of the sky.

A hand on hers cleared the fog in her mind. Bree blinked, finding Seamus's large, warm fingers wrapping the back of her hand. He sent her a look, not of sympathy, but understanding, his eyes quiet.

Nadine stuck her tweezers into Seamus's side. He clamped down on Bree's hand, then realized and tried to let go. Bree firmed her grip before he could pull away, holding on to him.

Clink. One bullet hit the tray. *Clink.* Another.

Seamus's golden gaze fixed on Bree, as though focusing on her eased the pain.

Clink.

"Now hold still," Nadine said as she picked out the tiny pellets. "If you were my boy, I'd give you stitches, but you're one of those Shifters, and who knows what would happen if I stuck a bunch of thread in you? I'll just bandage you up, but you'll need to stay quiet. No running around for a while."

Seamus moved with Feline restlessness, but he drew a breath and deliberately calmed himself as Nadine dabbed him with disinfectant. He also didn't let go of Bree's hand.

"Those guys chasing us did this, right?" Bree asked him. "Why were they shooting at you?"

"They're Shifter hunters." Seamus grunted as Nadine pulled at his wound. "Which means they'll be coming."

"This house is fairly isolated," Bree said. "That's why I brought you here—they'll never think to look out this way."

Seamus's eyes were filled with certainty. "I'm an un-Collared Shifter. Fair game. They'll look."

Bree supposed a very resourceful hunter would have taken down the make and model of her truck, maybe memorized her license plate and have a way to look it up at the department of motor vehicles.

She'd already obtained Texas plates for her truck, which would help with anonymity. There had to be several million pickups with Texas plates in this state. Or the hunters had gotten lucky and found the cell phone Seamus had tossed out into the darkness.

However, Bree understood from other Shifters that Shifter hunters weren't very bright. They were allowed to go after feral Shifters and the rare Shifter without a Collar, but Collared Shifters who followed the rules were off limits. Hunters, in truth, would take a shot at *any* Shifter, and claim later that they hadn't seen the Collar.

Seamus flinched again as Nadine pulled a bandage tightly around his torso. "You've done this a lot," he said to her.

Nadine returned the things to her box and carried the tweezers and anything bloody to the sink. She'd wash them then boil them and wipe them with alcohol. "You'd be amazed how many idiots with guns get themselves shot. Including my own son, God bless him."

Bree's emotions surged again, which she hid by quickly looking away.

"If you're a Shifter," Nadine said to Seamus from the sink. "Why don't you have one of those Collars?"

"*Mom.*" Bree raised her head to glare her mother to silence. "I was trying not to mention it."

"Well, we need to know." Nadine kept her attention her task. "I thought they all had to wear the Collars to keep them from turning into wild beasts or something."

Seamus had gone very still, and his eyes … changed. One moment they looked as human as Remy's, the next they'd flicked to the tawny, slit-pupilled eyes of a cat. A wild cat, holding himself quiet until he decided to strike.

"I won't hurt you," Seamus said.

"Damn right you won't." Nadine dried her hands and extracted another cigarette. "I just patched you up. It would be very bad manners."

Seamus still had hold of Bree's hand. His fingers tightened on hers, as though he worried she'd pull away and run.

Bree wasn't sure what she wanted to do. On the one hand, no Collar meant no shock devices to control Seamus if he went crazy violent and started to tear up the place. Collars were supposed to keep Shifters from reverting to their wild ways. A Shifter who'd never worn a Collar ...

She'd never seen a Shifter without one. Most Shifters had been Collared twenty and more years ago—those who hadn't were rumored to be dead and gone. But there Seamus sat, his neck clear and free of any chain.

On the other hand, Seamus had jumped into her pickup and forced Bree to drive him away. He'd essentially abducted her.

On the third hand, he hadn't hurt her, and he obviously needed help. Seamus held on to Bree not so much to keep her from running, but as though holding her soothed him. She'd heard that the touch of a mate could heal a Shifter.

On the fourth hand—Bree had no idea what to think. What the hell? If she'd been back in Louisiana, she'd have called someone in a Shiftertown—she'd made enough friends to get hold of one—and asked them what to do about a Shifter without a Collar sitting in her kitchen.

Bree hadn't had a chance to meet any Shifters here, which was why she'd gone out tonight. Here, she had no contacts, no friends, nothing. The emptiness of that kicked her in the gut.

Seamus broke the silence. "I've never had a Collar. I was separated from my clan when I was very young — they were taken, and I escaped."

Nadine opened her mouth, smoke curling out of it, to ask more questions, but Bree shook her head the slightest bit, and her mother subsided.

Seamus's matter-of-fact statements, which clearly hid much more, spoke to her. Seamus was alone, his family gone. He was hurt, down, scared, though a man like him would refuse to show it.

Bree knew about that loneliness, when you'd lost what you loved and wanted to curl up and hide until you stopped hurting. It never went away, that hurting.

"You can stay here tonight," Bree said quietly. "Mom will make up a bed for you on the couch. We won't say anything to anyone, all right? It wouldn't be hospitable. You're hurt, and you needed our help. In the morning, if you still think you need to go, you go. You were never here."

Nadine ran water from the sink and set a pot on the stove. "It's kind of an unwritten rule in the Fayette family. If you're under our roof, we take care of you, even if you're a fugitive."

Seamus caught Bree's gaze with his Shifter one, and Bree couldn't look away. His golden eyes bore flecks of green, the irises ringed with deeper gold.

Then his eyes changed to human again, and Seamus gave Bree a nod. "I am grateful."

Bree let out a breath she hadn't realized she'd been holding. Seamus didn't loosen his grip, and he didn't look away.

"Good." Nadine clattered her instruments into the pot. "Bree, get out some clean sheets."

***

Seamus lay on the couch in the dark, a sheet pulled up over his jeans to his bandaged chest. He was wide awake, staring at the living room ceiling. His bare feet stuck out over the end of the sofa, his frame too long for him to stretch out.

Bree had taken his ruined shirt away, darting into a laundry room off the kitchen to toss it into the washing machine. The bandage around Seamus's torso itched, but it was a hell of a lot better than the hot bullets in his side.

He owed these people his life. Bree had gotten him away from the hunters in the nick of time—giving him a crazy, wild ride. Nadine had competently removed the bullets, which would allow Seamus to heal cleanly. His Shifter metabolism might have closed flesh around the shots, but they could have festered. Shifters were tough to kill, but infection happened.

Directly above him, separated from him by the ceiling, Bree lay in her bed. Seamus sensed her with his entire being, imagined her breathing quietly, covers over her body. Her golden hair would be rumpled on her pillow, her hand curled under one cheek.

His heart beat faster, but Seamus tried to suppress the vision. He didn't have time for an amorous encounter right now, didn't matter that the simple act of holding Bree's hand had both aroused him and eased his pain.

Bree was not for him. Seamus had bigger things to worry about than cuddling up with a woman, no matter how enticing she was.

He smiled in the darkness. Bree wasn't a meek, weak creature. She'd make someone a good mate.

Seamus saw the deep sorrow in her. The brother, Remy, Bree spoke of, who was very obviously not here, was dead. Seamus recognized the grief in Bree's eyes and that of the mother. Photos in the living room showed a young man in a uniform. Probably Remy had been killed in one of the endless wars humans waged with one another. In every decade there was one, the new war usually segueing from the previous one.

Not that Shifters couldn't fight bloody battles when they had to. The time was coming, Seamus knew, when such a thing would have to happen again.

Far above him, Seamus heard a soft thump and a rustle. He was already wide awake, but his Shifter self woke up further.

The sound hadn't come from Bree's bedroom, or Nadine's. It came from higher, at the top of the house — the attic.

Quietly, Seamus pushed back the sheet and rose to his feet. The rustle came again, as though someone had gone up to look through the boxes of junk left above.

In silence, he flowed up the stairs, already knowing which steps creaked and how to avoid them. He wouldn't be able to avoid making noise pulling open the attic door, though, so if he couldn't be stealthy, he'd simply have to be quick.

Seamus crouched down on his heels, and in one movement, sprang the distance between floor and ceiling, shoving the door out of his way as he went. He caught the frame around the attic door and swung himself upward, half scrambling, half leaping into the attic. His feet found beams on which to land, his vision changing to his lion's as he looked around the pitch-dark space.

Across the attic was a wavering light, which brightened into one clear beam as Seamus looked at it. In that light he saw that boxes had been upended, books and papers strewn about.

Then the light winked abruptly out, bathing the room in darkness. A few papers fluttered to the floor.

"Shit!" came Bree's whispered voice. Seamus looked down, finding her directly beneath the attic's trap door. Bree's eyes were wide, her cheek lined with creases from her pillow. "Please don't tell me my mom's right, and there really is a ghost."

Chapter Four

Seamus slid back through the opening, bracing himself on the trapdoor's frame before letting go. He landed on the floor below, right next to Bree, who didn't move an inch.

She wore a thin shirt that reached to her knees, opaque enough that Seamus could see the shape of her limbs beneath it. She smelled of warmth and sleep.

Seamus didn't touch her — it was enough for now to be beside her, breathing her scent. "I don't know what it was," he said, keeping his voice quiet. "The light shorting out, maybe." He didn't truly believe that, and he was puzzled by it. He hadn't sensed danger, exactly, but it was odd.

Bree glanced at the dark space above them. "Well, close it up, will you? It gives me the creeps." Before Seamus could move to put the door back in place, Bree took a step closer to him.

"Are you all right?" she asked in a soft voice. "You should be keeping still." She touched Seamus's side, where the bullets had been.

The soreness there, which had been bugging Seamus as he tried to sleep, eased a bit. Bree's fingers were small, her fingertips smooth.

She kept her gaze on his side as she traced the bandage over the now-closing holes, ran her fingers along ribs that had been black with bruises. The bruises were a greeny yellow, and their soreness faded as Bree touched them.

Seamus lifted his hand and cupped her face. Bree started, then leaned into his touch, her cheeks flushing, eyes sweeping downward. Her plump features were small against his palm. Seamus ran his thumb across her cheekbone, liking the softness of her skin.

Bree took a long breath and let it out, the brush of it sending a wave of pleasure all the way down his body. Seamus moved his thumb over her cheekbone again, more firmly this time as he learned the feel of her.

Her eyes were soft, the blue of them almost black in the darkness. Seamus slid his fingertips across her brows, brushing over her lashes as he came back to her cheek.

Bree's throat moved. She touched his side again, near the wounds, then ran her fingers around the lines of his pectorals and up to his shoulders.

The leisurely touch had him burning more than if she'd jumped on him and borne him to the floor. Not that he'd mind if she did that. Seamus would cradle her against him, soothe her eagerness with slow kisses ...

Her fingers moved across his shoulders, Bree's gaze on the hollow of his throat, where a Collar was supposed to rest. She leaned forward the slightest bit and touched her tongue to his skin there.

Seamus started, his blood igniting. Her hair brushed his nose, the violets smell coming to him again. Wanting greater than he'd ever felt rushed through him. Seamus had been holding himself so tightly for so long, that loosening was going to kill him.

He closed his eyes, inhaled the goodness of Bree, and pressed a kiss to her hair.

I need this woman. I need her to hold me, to help calm this thing raging inside me. I need her to heal me, to make me whole again ...

There was a sudden clatter from Nadine's room, and she yanked open her door, not six feet from Seamus.

Bree wrenched herself away from him, her face flaming. The shock of her vanishing warmth jerked a growl from Seamus's throat. Time had slowed, thickening, as he'd touched her. Now it rolled forward with a kick.

"I heard it," Nadine said. She struggled to tie a robe around her substantial form. "What did I tell you? Seamus, help me get up there. I want a look."

***

Seamus at first refused. Too dangerous, he said. Bree privately agreed with him, but her mother wouldn't take no for an answer. Now Bree waited, heart beating rapidly, as Seamus maneuvered the ladder he'd brought from the garage under the hole.

Bree was on fire from his touch, her fingers tingling with the need to reach for him, to taste him again. His skin had been vibrant under her tongue, smooth, with a bite of salt. She'd never sensed the vitality, the *aliveness*, for want of a better word, in any other Shifter that she sensed in Seamus.

Maybe because he didn't have a Collar? Didn't have to curb himself to avoid pain as other Shifters did? Or was it something about *him*, Seamus himself?

All Bree knew was that if he'd led her back inside her bedroom, slid off her shirt, and made swift love to her on her bed, she wouldn't have stopped him. Would have encouraged him all the way. Still might.

Nadine snapped on the lights in the attic from the switch in the hall. Seamus had suggested it was the light shorting out up there that had caused the flickering, but nope. The light came on, beaming a small circle down at them.

Seamus started climbing the ladder, which looked rickety, though Nadine claimed it was perfectly good. As firmly as Seamus held it from above, Bree from below, it rocked around as Nadine scrambled up.

"Get up here, Bree," Nadine called down once Seamus had helped her into the attic. "Come and see. Don't worry; you'll be fine."

Seamus gave Bree a reassuring nod. Bree rolled her eyes and put her foot on the first rung.

The ladder shook, swayed, creaked, as she ascended. Bree didn't much like ladders, having fallen off one and broken her ankle when she was six. The ankle in question gave a throb, questioning her sanity.

Bree held her breath, clung to the ladder, and made it to the top. Seamus caught her hands and steadied her as she stepped from the ladder onto the beams of the attic.

There was plenty of room to stand up, Bree found as she straightened, the roof peaking high above them. The closely spaced floor beams were the sturdiest things to stand on, though boards had been laid between them.

Keeping her feet on the beams, Bree carefully made her way to where her mother was picking up papers from beside a box. "This is what he was looking at," Nadine said. "This is what fell."

She thrust the papers at Bree. Bree found herself looking at a copy of Remy's orders from the army and his paperwork from after he'd been killed. The box held a few books and things he'd saved from high school—his yearbook, a boutonniere his girlfriend had given him at his last Homecoming dance, racing car posters that had hung in his room, complete with buxom females draped over said cars.

"It was Remy," Nadine said, beaming. "He was looking for something. These are his things."

"You stuffed Remy's things up here in the attic?" Bree looked at her mother in surprise. After Remy's death, Nadine and Bree had been very careful with anything he'd ever touched. When they'd moved into this two-bedroom house, Nadine had fitted out the closet between the bedrooms with shelves and neatly placed the things they'd kept in it—photos, T-shirts, letters, Remy's uniforms, trinkets that had been special to him. Paperwork was in a strongbox.

"No, I didn't," Nadine said, scowling. "Do you think I would? Don't you see? *He* must have brought them here."

"Mom." Bree folded her arms. She was still swaying from Seamus touching her with the gentlest hands. She'd not been able to resist touching him in return—his side, then his chest, feeling solid muscle dusted with golden hair, his heart beating beneath his bones.

Her mother insisting that Remy's ghost was up here, come back to see them for whatever reason, wasn't helping Bree regain her equilibrium. The fact that Seamus waited quietly as she and her mother played out the drama, silent and upright like a sentinel, didn't help either.

"It wasn't Remy," Bree said in a hard voice. "He's gone."

Nadine was unfazed. "Who was it then? Of course Remy would want his things."

Bree started to answer then broke off. She knew her mother was still grieving, as Bree was. Not long after Remy's death, Nadine had gone to a psychic near their little town in Louisiana, a woman who'd taken her money to let her receive messages from Remy on the other side.

When Bree—and the police—had proved the woman a fraud, Nadine hadn't been angry with the psychic. Talking to Remy had comforted her, she'd said. Just because that psychic had been bogus didn't mean the supernatural didn't exist. And anyway, didn't Bree have a thing for people who could turn into animals?

Bree had conceded the point, but even so, tried to discourage her from believing Remy was trying to communicate with them. She wondered if her mom had put these things up here, to build the fiction that Remy was looking out for them. Perhaps she'd "prove" it and feel better.

But Remy was gone, as much as Bree hated to keep saying it. They needed to learn to accept it, and move on. Maybe then the pain would lessen—though Bree doubted it.

Seamus came out of his silent stance and moved toward the boxes, looking like a fertility god of old with his well-muscled, bare torso, even with the bandages. Nadine started, as though she'd forgotten he was with them.

"Do you want me to take the things downstairs?" Seamus offered. His voice was quiet, understanding.

Nadine blinked, her eyes wet. Then she frowned and put on her usual no-nonsense expression, which she did when she needed to pull herself back to the present. "You can't be lifting boxes after you've been shot." She looked him up and down. "Though you seem a lot better. I guess Shifters really do heal fast." She shook her head. "No. Let's straighten up but leave everything here. I'm sure Remy put it here for a reason. If he comes back, maybe he'll tell me why."

Bree exchanged a glance with Seamus, who gave her the slightest shake of head. It was an interesting day—or night—when a wild Shifter without a Collar who'd kidnapped Bree and was now hiding out with her made more sense than Bree's messed-up life.

"We can straighten it out tomorrow, Mom," Bree said, trying to sound soothing. "I'll make some tea, and then we'll go back to bed."

Seamus had already started lifting the strewn papers and books and setting them neatly back into the boxes. Nadine must be tired, because she let him.

"Good idea," Nadine said, sounding weary. "A nice herbal tea, maybe with a little shot, so I'll sleep nice and cozy."

Seamus finished and went down the ladder first. He didn't use every rung; his lithe body moved quickly downward, sliding the last yard with his bare feet on either side of the ladder. He betrayed no awareness of his nimbleness—he was comfortable with his body, not showing off.

He held the ladder as first Nadine then Bree descended. Seamus put his hands on Bree's waist to lift her down the last few feet, his grip strong. Bree leaned into him, as she had when he'd touched her so tenderly, before her mother had interrupted. She hadn't mistaken the need in his eyes then, and she didn't mistake it now.

Seamus's hands compressed the slightest bit on her sides, a hidden caress. Bree drew a breath, trying not to like that so much.

Seamus released her and turned away to carry the ladder downstairs. Bree watched his tight back, which was crisscrossed with scars, as he went down, hoisting the ladder as though it weighed nothing.

Nadine snapped off the attic light. "Bree."

Bree jerked her gaze from Seamus as he disappeared through the door to the garage, where the ladder was stored. "What?"

"He's good looking." Nadine appeared wrung out, but her voice was as steely as ever. "He's sexy without knowing it, and you're lonely. But he's Shifter, and there's something wrong with him, more than just the fact that he doesn't have one of those Collars. He seems different from the other Shifters I've seen, and not only because of the Collar thing."

"I know." Bree sighed. "All that. I know."

Nadine put a hand Bree's shoulder. "I just don't want to see you get hurt, honey. You've done enough hurting for three women your age. In the morning, Seamus will want to move on. You let him go."

Bree shivered in her thin nightshirt, in spite of her mother's warm touch, but she knew Nadine was right. Seamus had needed help tonight, he'd chosen Bree to help him, and then he'd leave. He couldn't risk being caught without a Collar.

Seamus came in from the garage. Nadine went on down the stairs past him to the kitchen, and Bree quickly followed her. She didn't trust herself alone with Seamus, so she was right behind her mother as they entered the kitchen for their soothing cups of spiked tea.

***

When Seamus awoke in the morning, back on the couch and tangled in sheets, the tabby cat was lying on his ankles.

It always amazed him, Seamus thought as he carefully sat up and stroked the blinking cat between its ears, how heavy very small cats could be.

The cat yawned, stretched, poked its needle claws through the sheet, and kneaded Seamus's bare leg. He'd taken off the jeans this time, lying down to sleep after he'd cleaned up the best the bandages would let him in the tub upstairs.

Seamus pried the cat up, detaching it from the sheet, and cradled it against his chest. The cat, knowing a sucker when she saw one, purred and soaked up the petting.

It was early, around five thirty, Seamus judged from the gray light. It was autumn, November, and the sun wouldn't be up for a little bit yet. No one stirred above—Seamus had the feeling that Nadine and Bree weren't women who shot out of bed at the crack of dawn.

He looked forward to seeing Bree stumbling down the stairs, mussed from her sleep, giving him her lopsided smile.

Strange, Seamus had all his life feared and even hated humans. They were physically weaker than Shifters and yet had manipulated themselves to have mastery of this world. Their animal strength had been replaced by cunning, which in the long run had proved the more capable trait for them. If you knew exactly how fast to run and precisely where to hide from the stronger, stupider predators, you could outlast them.

This cat had the same kind of cunning. Her ancestors had been quick and resourceful, and had discovered that being adorably cute had its benefits. A dangerous Shifter who could have made short work of this cat was now cuddling it, protecting it, making it feel good.

The cat suddenly lifted her head, her claws coming out to bury themselves in Seamus's muscular arm. He tensed but didn't drop her or toss her away.

An animal coming alert meant something Seamus couldn't ignore. His own senses prickled.

Seamus very carefully set the cat on the floor then raised his head, parted the sheer curtain of the living room window, and peered out.

The house was surrounded by Shifters.

Chapter Five

Seamus very slowly eased back down to the sofa and reached for the clean, whole, olive-green T-shirt Nadine had brought him—belonging to her son, he understood. Seamus slid it on and then his jeans. He didn't bother with his boots, because if he had to shift and fight, boots would only get in the way.

He didn't recognize the Shifters out there, but he knew who they must be. How they'd tracked him here, Seamus didn't know, but Collared Shifters were crafty, like the humans he'd just been thinking of.

Seamus needed to be just as crafty himself. He had to get away from the Shifters but also not allow them to follow him to those he was protecting. *Keep them safe. That is the mission.*

Dressed, he quietly made for the front door and crouched against the wall beside it. He couldn't fight them all, but he could lead them astray and then find a way to slip around them and make his escape. Maybe. Getting away from Shifters wasn't as easy as evading trigger-happy humans.

The Shifters outside were deathly silent. They only had to wait it out, and they knew it.

From somewhere above him, a window scraped open. A second later, Nadine yelled, "Get off my property, all of you, or eat lead!"

Shite. Seamus was across the room and up the stairs in an instant, going on all fours to keep his head down.

He nearly slammed into Bree on the landing. She was indeed mussed and warm from sleep, her hair tousled, her eyes bleary. "What the hell is going on?" she asked in confusion. "Mom, what are you *doing*?"

Nadine, in a robe, her bleached hair sticking out every which way, was standing at her bedroom window overlooking the front of the house, shotgun in hand.

"I'm about to shoot some Shifters who've decided to camp out on my lawn." Nadine said testily. "You all back off!" she called down to them. "All the way to the street. Or I call the cops."

None of the Shifters moved. Nadine lifted the shotgun, sighted, and pulled the trigger.

The *boom* of the gun rocketed through Seamus's senses. Bree screamed and clapped her hands over her ears. The cat, who'd followed them, streaked from this bedroom and into Bree's.

Outside, there was shouting, a couple of the Shifters boiling apart from where Nadine had aimed. She hadn't hit any, Seamus saw from a quick glance. She'd shot at the ground, a warning.

Seamus positioned the mirror on Nadine's dresser so that he could see out the window without any of the Shifters below being able to see him. He counted four in front of the house. Probably the same number were in back, with more out of sight on the perimeter. That's how he would have positioned his trackers.

Seamus knew who the leader was, the one who stepped forward, his hands raised in a placating gesture. Not surrender — this Shifter didn't know the meaning of the word.

"I know you have a Shifter in there," the man said, his rumbling voice carrying. The hint of Irish accent was clear. "Send him out, and we go home. We have no wish to harm you."

Seamus had never met Dylan Morrissey, but he knew a lot about him. All Shifters did. The man used to be leader of the Austin Shiftertown. When his son took over, Dylan became more of an overseer, roaming the Shifter territories in South Texas, making sure all Shifters kept in line. Rogue and feral Shifters were to be rounded up, brought in, Collared, and processed. Dylan and his trackers did a lot of that.

Dylan had been instrumental in shutting down the bunker that had housed Kendrick and his Shifters. He'd destroyed it and left Kendrick's Shifters in the wind. Dark anger spiraled inside him.

"You're still on my property," Nadine shouted down. "Now get the hell off it. Want me to have you rounded up and caged?"

Dylan didn't move. He was flanked by a man with a sword—a Guardian. Probably his son, Sean Morrissey, the Guardian of the Austin Shiftertown.

The very large Shifter standing behind the two of them had to be a bear. Only bears had that much bulk. The fourth was tall and hard, with tattoos all over him, his head shaved.

Trackers, Seamus surmised, and tough ones. The bear would be stronger than all of them put together but not as fast. The Morrisseys were lions, like Seamus—he'd be more or less evenly matched against each of them individually, though Dylan had a rep of never being beaten.

Seamus wasn't sure about the tatt guy. Feline by the look of him, but Seamus couldn't tell what kind of cat he was. If something like cheetah, then the guy could outrun Seamus but probably not outfight him. The guy looked like he could hold his own, however. He radiated self-assurance.

A fifth Shifter walked around the house to join them. He was big like the bear, but with close-cut black hair, tatts, and an attitude that could only be Lupine.

Dylan tried again. "We can scent the Shifter. Tell him to come out, and we'll be gone."

"I don't know what you're talking about," Nadine said. "You get off my property, *then* we'll talk."

Dylan made a minute signal to the trackers. Nadine and Bree wouldn't catch it, but Seamus recognized the body language. It was, *Find a way in and take him.*

Seamus turned from the mirror, though he remained out of sight of the windows. "I'll go down," he said quietly to Nadine and Bree. "I don't want them to hurt you." Not that he planned to submit without a fight. He'd go, but they'd have to catch him.

Seamus suited action to word, without waiting for response, heading for the stairs.

A soft body brushed by, and then Bree was in front of him, blocking his way. "Like hell you're giving yourself up." Bree scowled, blue eyes glittering with anger. "They might be Shifters, but they don't look like they want to hand you a beer and welcome you with open arms."

Seamus put his hand on her shoulder. *Damn, damn, damn.* He shouldn't have done that—one touch, and he didn't want to let go. He wanted to stay here, sink into Bree's softness, let her make his troubles melt away. Or at least give him the illusion that his troubles no longer existed. Let him float in pure bliss.

But if he didn't leave, Bree might be hurt, and so could others who depended on him. He didn't know what the Shifters outside would do to Bree and Nadine if they came storming in to grab Seamus. While Shifters were usually careful with humans, they did so mostly to avoid drawing the attention of the human police and Shifter Bureau. They weren't necessarily kind.

"I didn't say I'd give up," Seamus told Bree, reluctantly lifting his hand away. "I'll distract them and run. Draw them away from you."

At the window, Nadine said, "Oh, I'll give them a distraction."

Not a bad idea. "Wait until I'm ready," Seamus said. "I'll signal, you do your thing, and I'll go."

He pushed around Bree and went down the stairs but heard her coming behind him.

"*Seamus.*" Bree grabbed the tail of his shirt. Seamus turned back, caught more by her presence than her hold. "You can't."

"I can," Seamus said. "I'm fast. I'll be gone before they realize."

"That's not what I meant. What will they do to you if they catch you?"

"They're from the Austin Shiftertown," Seamus said—no reason for her not to know. "They want to put a Collar on me and sequester me. They've been chasing me ... us ... for about a month now."

Bree tightened her hand on the T-shirt's hem. "Where will you go?"

"Somewhere   not   here,"   Seamus   said. "Understand? They'll chase *me* away from *you*. It's what I do. You and your mother don't need a bunch of pain in the ass Shifters giving you grief."

Bree's blue eyes took on a bleak look. Without the makeup, waking up from sleep, Seamus saw that she was a little older than he'd first thought—not that he was an expert on human ages. She was old enough to have a mate and cub of her own, old enough to have had life kick at her.

Bree took a step closer to him. "What I mean is, will I ever see you again?"

Seamus studied her for a few beats. In that moment, his body, which had been cooperative up until now, became a massive knot of pain.

He'd been calmer since he'd been in this house, giving him a crumb of hope that he'd conquered the wildness bubbling inside him. He realized as Bree's body brushed his, that he'd conquered it because of *her*. As soon as he'd found her, her nearness, her touch had started to quiet him down.

If he left her, would the pain, the confusion, come rushing back?

But if Seamus stayed, he'd leave Bree open to danger. No matter what, Seamus had to go.

Seamus peeled Bree's hold from his shirt, wrapped his arm around her, and dragged her close. Warmth of woman came to him as Bree's body curved against his, the thin shirt letting him feel her limbs, her full breasts, the supple bend of her spine.

Seamus leaned down and kissed her mouth, a full kiss, not preparing her, not going slowly. He needed to kiss her right now, might never have another chance.

Bree curled her fists on his shoulders but didn't push away. She opened her lips to him, accepting. Her tongue moved against his, she tasting him, pushing herself up into him.

Seamus deepened the kiss, taking what he could. Bree tasted of spice and the night, heat and everything that was good. He tasted her deep sorrow as well, a sadness she couldn't shake, and her need. Bree had so much need. She was hungry, this woman, and no one had filled that craving within her.

Pain snatched at him and wouldn't relent. Seamus could take her with him, keep her next to him, whatever happened. Bound as one, mates.

He tightened his embrace, kissing her harder. Bree answered with as bold a kiss. She needed him, and he her. Primal, basic need.

Bree wrapped her arms around his neck, her unfettered breasts scooping against him. Bree's back was a pliant line, drawing his hands along it to her buttocks. Soft flesh met his touch, their position rubbing her abdomen right over his cock.

If five and more Shifters hadn't been ready to charge the house and break down the door, Seamus would have lowered Bree to the stairs and relieved his frenzy then and there. Swift thrusts while she clung to him, the sounds Bree made in her throat escalating to full cries as they reached the breaking point together.

For now, Seamus could only touch her, kiss her, drink in her warmth against the coldness that was to come.

"Any time you're ready, Seamus."

Nadine's quiet voice came from above. Bree abruptly broke the kiss, her eyes wide, face flushed, her breathing rapid.

Nadine peered over the banisters at them, the shotgun held carefully so the barrel pointed upward.

Seamus turned his back and walked away, moving on down the stairs. If he stayed, if he looked at Bree one second longer, he'd never go, and he knew it.

***

Bree had forgotten how to breathe, talk, maybe even stand. She held herself up against the wall, trying to find her balance, while her entire body rejoiced at the kiss.

Seamus had held her like a lover, as though they'd been together for years instead of meeting for the first time last night under dire circumstances. His kiss had been hot, strong, thorough, hinting at what fever could be had from a night in bed with him.

Above him, her mother was watching in disapproval. Bree couldn't raise her head to look up at Nadine, but the weight of the disapproval was like a blanket dropping on her head.

Worse still was the cold slap of Seamus walking away. He was running from her into danger—no way could he evade that bunch of scary-looking Shifters waiting for him outside.

Bree shoved herself away from the wall and ran on shaking legs after him.

From the kitchen, Seamus yelled, "Nadine ... *now!*"

Her mother must have gotten herself back in position, because the shotgun went off twice—*bang! bang!* Next came a few moments of silence while Nadine reloaded, then the gun went off again.

The Shifters outside were shouting. Bree hit the kitchen in time to see Seamus slip out the back door. Bree ran to the door and sheltered herself behind it while she looked out into the dawn.

Seamus had already vanished. One smudge of dirt on the wooden steps showed he'd passed, but where he'd gone, Bree couldn't see.

Her heart wrenched, her extremities going numb. When they'd gotten word about Remy, she'd felt a bit like this—the entire world changing while she stood there, unable to stop it. She'd lost Remy, and she was losing Seamus, and there wasn't a damn thing she could do about it.

A roar like that of a primeval beast rolled across the field beyond the house. It caught Bree, vibrated the windows, shook the porch. Another roar answered it, this one different, quicker, touched with rage.

A lion came bounding out of the field. It had a black mane, a lithe muscular frame, giant paws, and tawny eyes. Lion eyes. Seamus's eyes.

Right behind it was the biggest Bengal tiger Bree had ever seen in her life. Not that she'd seen many, but she'd stood by their enclosures in zoos. Those tigers had been big and intimidating enough—this tiger was gigantic.

And furious. His ears were flat on his head, his eyes a wild gold. Within two bounds, it was on the lion—Seamus—who turned and fought for his life.

Another lion raced around the house. This one too had a black mane, but it was larger, older, with massive confidence in his eyes. He ran right between the tiger and Seamus, planting his feet and barking a roar that pounded in Bree's ears. Seamus roared an answer, but the tiger went deathly silent.

The tiger, his eyes still sparking anger, retreated a few steps, turned in a slow circle, and stood poised, ready to spring. The tiger could have wiped out both lions with one sweep of his big paws, but now he simply waited, watching. Almost like he was being *polite*.

The older lion, on the other hand, was advancing on Seamus, mouth curling with his snarls, the intent in his eyes unmistakable.

Give up, or we kill you.

"*No!*" Bree shouted.

She was out of the house, down the steps, and running to them before she realized what she was doing. She stopped in front of Seamus and faced the other lion, whose growls increased.

"No," Bree repeated, trying to catch her breath. She was scared shitless—the lion Shifter was gigantic, mean-looking, and could kill her without breaking a sweat. Not only that, but the tiger could come behind him and stamp out whatever bits of her were left.

Seamus was snarling, trying to push her aside with his body, but Bree stayed put.

"You leave him alone," she yelled at the older lion. "Understand me? You go away, and leave him *alone*." Bree took the final step to the second lion and smacked him hard across the nose.

Chapter Six

What the holy hell was she doing?

The words flitted through a corner of Seamus's brain, along with a surge of frustrated rage. A stronger anger and incredulity washed after that, emotions flying so fast the confusion made him blink.

Then his mind cleared, leaving only one sharp, focused idea: *Protect*.

Seamus had already shoved himself between Bree and Dylan, his ears back, snarls unceasing. He'd go for Dylan the moment Dylan put a paw toward Bree, didn't matter that Dylan was an alpha and one of the most dominant Shifters Seamus had ever encountered.

This was different. This was a *mate* thing.

Seamus saw that acknowledgment in Dylan's eyes behind the absolute fury. Dylan stood his ground, neither continuing the attack nor backing off.

Bree, damn her, was trying to push herself in front of Seamus again. "He isn't hurting you," she yelled at Dylan. "Or me. Or anyone. What the hell do you want from him?"

Seamus turned his growls on her. Bree needed to stay behind him, let him defend her. Dylan had conceded the mate idea, with a flash of surprise, but that didn't mean he might not swat Bree to the ground to make her shut up.

Bree only drew another breath to continue berating Dylan. At that moment, the tiger shifted smoothly into a huge man with mottled red-orange and black hair and golden eyes. He wrapped giant arms around Bree, lifted her from her feet, and carried her aside, Bree flailing and protesting all the way.

The Lupine, the Guardian, the bear, and the tattooed guy had come around the house, still in their humans forms.

"Stand down," the Guardian growled at Seamus, his accent as Irish as Dylan's. "We're trying to help you, man."

The Lupine, in a muscle shirt and jeans, folded his arms. "Yeah, we can do this the hard way, or we can do this the *hard* way." He broke off and chuckled. "I've always wanted to say that."

"And all of you can back off!" Bree shouted at them.

She'd stopped fighting—the tiger held her firmly—but she wasn't about to be quiet. Seamus both admired that and found it worrying.

Nadine burst out of the back door, her shotgun ready. "This might not kill Shifters," she said in a firm voice. "But I've seen the damage it can cause. Anyone want to spend the day getting pellets picked out of them?"

"Mom, go back inside!" Bree cried in alarm.

Nadine cocked the gun, pointing it at the tiger. "And I *really* don't like naked men trampling my garden. Let my daughter go."

The tiger-man looked at Dylan then at Nadine. Finally, he focused his all-tiger stare on Seamus. Dylan snarled at him, clearly telling the Bengal to keep hold of Bree.

The tiger waited a few more heartbeats, then he slowly released Bree, setting her on her feet. He turned his back on them all, flowed into his tiger form, and walked away, huffing under his breath.

Seamus had never seen a Shifter so easily change shape before. Seamus had struggled with the shift mightily as a cub, finding it painful until he grew into it. Even now the shift was tough for him. Kendrick was much better at it, able to change nearly as instantaneously as this Bengal. Maybe it was a tiger thing.

Nadine wasn't finished. "Now, the rest of you, get back into whatever vehicles brought you here and go. I won't ask you again."

The Guardian, sunlight catching on his sword's hilt, took a few cautious steps toward her. "I would, lass, but that big lion is my dad, and he'll never let me hear the end of it if I don't finish this. We just want to take *this* Shifter back home with us. He won't be hurt. He's one of us."

Bree rounded on the Guardian, her fists clenched. "How can you say he won't be hurt? You'll put a Collar on him and keep him in Shiftertown. Why would you want to do that? He hasn't done anything wrong."

"Oh," the Lupine said with a low growl. "I like her."

The bear rumbled next to him. "Me too."

The Guardian didn't join their mirth. His eyes were stern as he regarded Bree. "Last night a feral Shifter ripped apart two human hunters. We got word that more hunters were chasing a Shifter they saw at the scene—all evidence we found points to that Shifter being *him*." He jerked a thumb at Seamus. "We need to contain this before the human police come after him."

Bree's mouth dropped open, and Nadine blinked.

Bree recovered. "He didn't kill anyone," she said hotly. "Seamus was with us all last night. He had coffee, slept on the couch. The hunters were chasing Seamus, not the other way around."

"Seamus is his name, is it?" the Guardian asked. "Seamus McGuire?"

Bree looked at him blankly—Seamus had never told her his family name. That the Guardian knew it didn't surprise Seamus all that much. Guardians had a secret database that listed all Shifters—names, locations, details—accessible only by Guardians.

The Lupine growled at Seamus. "That's you, right, Feline?"

"What evidence?" Bree interrupted. "It had better be good."

The Guardian pulled a small object from his pocket. "Seamus at one point had his hand on this. We found it not far from where a truck had been parked. It belongs to you."

Bree stared in surprise. "That's my cell phone."

He didn't give it to her. "Indeed, it is. Witnesses said a Shifter got himself into your truck, the phone flew out, and the truck stormed away, chased by another full of humans. The phone has Seamus's scent and a bit of his blood on it, not to mention his fingerprints, and the last call was listed as coming from your mum. Not hard after that to trace you back here." He showed a hint of smile. "Not for a Guardian, anyway."

Dylan could have shifted back to human and joined the discussion, but he stayed animal. Smart— it gave him the best chance to take down Seamus if Seamus tried to run. The tiger remained in his beast form as well, but he was walking the boundary, not listening to the conversation.

Seamus knew that the minute he shifted to human, they'd take him. He couldn't fight them all, even if he remained in big cat form, but they seemed to think he was at bay for now.

His advantage—they had Collars, and Seamus did not.

Seamus didn't wait to calculate trajectory, speed, whatever. If he did, Dylan would sense it, and be all over him before he could take one step.

So he simply ran. One moment he was in a defensive posture against Dylan, claws dug into the dirt, the next, he was running.

His only thought was to lead them far away. They'd chase Seamus, leave Bree alone. Bree wasn't stupid — she'd take her mother to safety as soon as the Shifters came after him.

Texas weeds and dirt tore loose under his feet, billowing up a concealing cloud. Seamus increased his speed, making for the open fields that led to rolling hill country ...

... and found a giant Bengal tiger pinning him down.

Damn, the tiger was strong and fecking *fast*. Tiger paws crushed Seamus's back, and a mouth with massive teeth closed around his neck. Nothing broke the skin, but he had Seamus flat. Seamus wasn't going anywhere anytime soon.

Dylan came jogging up, in his human form now. He was strong-bodied, with dark hair going gray at the temples, and blue eyes that had observed much for many years.

"Shift," Dylan ordered.

His dominance was so complete that Seamus started to obey before he stopped himself. The Tiger still had his paws firmly on Seamus's back, the pressure of which would crush his human form.

"Tiger, ease off," Dylan said. "Seamus, I need you able to talk to me."

Seamus didn't give a damn. He didn't want to talk, he wanted to get the hell away from here.

What sold him was the fact that the bear had caught hold of Bree. He held her loosely, not hurting her, but his stance told Seamus that he knew how to contain people, no matter what they tried.

Behind them, the big Lupine had started for Nadine, his hands up, as though in surrender. While he pretended to come at her peacefully, Tatt Man slid silently behind Nadine and had the shotgun out of her arms before she understood what was happening. Felines could be damn stealthy.

Tatt-Man uncocked the shotgun, and the Lupine blew out a breath. "Thanks, Spike."

Nadine turned on Spike, lunging for the gun, but the Lupine caught and held her in an easy grip. "Not so fast, Mom. Let's go inside, and you can make us coffee."

"Fuck you!" Nadine stated.

The Lupine looked amused. "You know, you remind me of my aunt."

The bear pulled his attention back from them. "I'm Ronan," he said to Bree. "The full-of-himself Lupine is Broderick, then we have Spike with the tattoos, Sean with the sword, and ... Tiger. He's just called Tiger. Dylan's the other lion who likes to tell people what to do."

Bree folded her arms, not caring. "Nice to meet you, Ronan. Now, get lost."

"We can't do that, lass," Sean said. "We really are here to help Seamus. If he didn't do the murders, fine and good. If he did—we have to figure out why and what to do before the human police get here and take him."

Bree hesitated. Seamus felt the indecision pouring off her—the need to believe Seamus had nothing to do with it warring with her fears that maybe he had.

Seamus would love to reassure her, but he still couldn't remember what had happened. Easy enough to recall a moment of wild, hot triumph, the taste of blood, the mad snarling, then the need to run and the pain of the shots. Hitting the parking lot of the roadhouse, searching for escape, and finding Bree waiting ...

Seamus shifted, his muscles stretching and aching as he moved again to human form. "All right," he said as he straightened to his full height, his voice still holding the growl of his lion. "Let's go inside, and talk. But no matter what I did, leave Bree and Nadine out of it. They had nothing to do with anything."

Dylan watched him a moment, then gave him a nod. "Understood. Ronan, Spike, Broderick, cover the outside. Nadine ..." He pinned Nadine with an alpha stare, which apparently did not impress her. "May we enter your house?"

***

Bree watched her mother weigh the pros and cons of letting the Shifters talk versus trying to grab the shotgun back from Spike and opening fire. Nadine hated obeying orders, especially from men. Back in her younger days, Nadine hadn't had to fight for her rights as a woman—she'd simply taken them, to hell with anyone who got in her way.

Finally, Nadine shrugged and headed into the house. She wanted to know what was going on as much as Bree did.

Bree went straight to Seamus. He'd shifted from lion to human before her eyes and now stood tall in the dust and weeds beyond their small yard without a stitch on. He'd been hot enough in only his jeans, but now ...

The bandages had ripped away when he'd shifted—pieces lay scattered across the patch of lawn behind the house. The bruises on his ribs had faded, the holes where the bullets had been, now small, red marks.

Seamus betrayed no embarrassment being unclothed in front of Bree or the others. From what Bree had learned, Shifters were more animal in their emotions than human—shifting was natural, nothing to be ashamed of.

Bree saw nothing at *all* to shame him. Seamus's thighs were tight under flat, hard abs, and what hung between those thighs made her break into a sweat. Shifters were bigger than human men, in all ways. Seriously.

Bree realized she was staring and raised her gaze from his nether regions, but Seamus had seen. From the look on his face, he didn't mind.

Behind his mild satisfaction that she liked looking at him, Bree read need in his eyes, and despair, and deep fear. Seamus was afraid he truly had killed the hunters, Bree saw, and the idea haunted him.

"I don't remember," he said fiercely. He looked directly at Bree, no one else. "I don't remember anything. Only fighting something, running hard and fast, the shots, the roadhouse, and then you."

Bree stepped closer to him, the ground cold and sharp under her bare feet, and closed her hands around his forearms. "I won't let them take you away." She looked straight up into his face, willing him to believe her. "I won't let them lock you up for something you didn't do."

Seamus's golden eyes glittered in the morning light. "I don't *know* if I didn't do it."

"Come inside," Bree said softly. "We'll find out."

Seamus kept his gaze on her, in spite of the other Shifters drifting to circle them—Dylan wasn't about to let him get away again. Only he and Bree might be standing there in the Texas dawn, a cold breeze plucking at them, while the rest of the Shifters, the house, the sign in the field promising a new development coming soon—the sign had been there for five years, their neighbors had told them—the entire world, floated away.

Bree gave Seamus's arms a squeeze. His skin was hot, smooth over muscle, satin over steel. Seamus stood impossibly still while his eyes betrayed that, inside, he was one mass of pain.

Bree remembered when he'd first jumped into her truck, the wildness in his eyes, the anger, the fear.

Are you feral? she'd asked him.

Maybe, he'd answered distractedly. *Not yet ...*

But he feared he was becoming so. A feral Shifter might not remember that he'd killed two men and fled, coming to himself long enough to force a woman in a truck to help him get away.

"I won't let you," Bree told him, her voice firm. "I won't let you be feral. Understand me?"

Seamus only watched her, whatever thoughts warring in his mind making his eyes fill with fear, his skin bead with sweat.

He abruptly closed his hands over her arms in return, his large fingers folding around her. "I need ..."

Whatever he needed, he couldn't express with speech. His hands bit down, the grip tight, and mercilessly strong.

But not to hurt her—Seamus was trying to hold on to something that wasn't whirling, rushing, and tumbling over him. Bree met his gaze, wanting to tell him she believed in him, was there for him, but not finding the right words.

He didn't need words, she realized. Her touch was enough.

Behind Bree, Ronan was rumbling in his deep voice. "I think it's too late for an investigation, Dylan. They're coming."

Ronan didn't specify who *they* were, but there wasn't much mistaking the sirens that wailed across the fields and from the end of the drive to the house.

Dylan had pulled on jeans and a button-down shirt. "Inside," he commanded. *"Now."*

Seamus grabbed Bree's hand and hustled her across the damp lawn toward the house, sweeping up the pile of his clothes on the way. Bree stumbled up the steps and into the kitchen as the harsh sound of sirens coated the air.

Chapter Seven

"Seriously—who called the cops?" Nadine demanded as Seamus and Bree, Dylan, Sean, and Tiger entered the kitchen. Dylan closed the door behind them and locked it. The other Shifters had faded from sight outside, blending into the early gray light.

Bree's heart was pounding. Seamus still had hold of her hand. They were bound together through the clasp, as though Seamus wouldn't go feral as long as they didn't part.

Spike had handed Dylan the shotgun. Dylan popped the cartridges out and gave the unloaded gun back to Nadine. She took it, tight-lipped, but locked the gun into the cabinet inside the basement door. She wasn't foolish enough to go waving it around in front of police—well, not again, anyway. A night in jail in Louisiana had cured her of that.

"Who, is a good question," Dylan said. He moved to the front room, his words trailing behind him.

Seamus released Bree to resume his clothes, but he didn't move far from her. He was settling the T-shirt as Sean unstrapped the sword from his back.

The sword was gigantic, with a broad hilt, and looked very old. Letters Bree couldn't decipher were etched on the hilt and the crosspiece, running down into the sheath.

The Sword of the Guardian, Bree knew, though she'd never seen one. The blade was driven through the heart of a Shifter who'd died or was dying, to turn his or her body to dust and release the soul to the Summerland, the afterlife.

This sword, which looked ancient, must have gone through many Shifters in its time. Bree took a step back as Sean held it across both hands, and she noticed that Seamus did as well.

"Will ye lock this in yon cabinet with your weapons, lass?" Sean asked Nadine. "Can't be letting the cops get hold of it."

Nadine heaved a sigh and beckoned him to follow. Sean went with her to the basement door.

Dylan returned to the kitchen. Bree couldn't see the other Shifters outside, but then, Shifters were good at hiding themselves.

The easiest thing Dylan could do was hand off Seamus to the cops. He could claim that Nadine and Bree had been Seamus's hostages, and Dylan and his Shifters had come here to rescue them and take Seamus in themselves.

Everyone would be happy, except Seamus, who'd be tranqued and taken away, likely to be put into a cage and then terminated. Bree was well aware what humans did to Shifters who were considered dangerous.

Bree sent Dylan a narrow look. "Don't you dare. You don't even know if he's guilty."

Dylan ignored her. He'd taken what looked like a chain from his pocket, and now he dangled it in front of Seamus.

The chain was of silver and black metal, woven into thick links. At its end hung a pendant, the Celtic knot, which would rest against Seamus's throat. Dylan wore an identical chain, as did all the Shifters here. A Collar.

Seamus's face went gray. "No, I can't."

"Suck it up and put it on," Dylan said sternly. "The police can't see you without one."

"It's fake." The slow growl of Tiger's voice filled the room. The big man with eyes as golden as Seamus's touched the Celtic knot on his own Collar. "Like mine."

Sean returned to them as Nadine moved behind him and, of all things, started making coffee. "That's supposed to be a secret, big guy," Sean said to Tiger.

"They need to know," Tiger answered.

Fake? Seamus was studying the Collar in grave suspicion. It sure looked real to Bree, no different than the ones around Sean's or Dylan's necks ... and even Tiger's.

Bree went cold as she realized the implications of what Tiger had said — his Collar wasn't real. That meant there was nothing to stop him from becoming that huge Bengal again and tearing into everyone, including Dylan.

Come to think of it, when Tiger had jumped on Seamus to bring him down, his Collar hadn't sparked. The Collars were supposed to, whenever a Shifter started to seriously fight. It would jerk pain through the Shifter's entire nervous system, shutting him down.

Bree and her groupie friends knew good and well that the Shifters had adapted to that pain—had to or it would have killed them long ago. They could fight each other at the illegal and secret fight clubs, ignoring the Collars the best they could to battle it out within the rings.

The fight clubs had *some* rules—no killing was the biggest one. Second biggest, fights were for exhibition only. Their outcomes did not change a Shifter's place in the dominance hierarchy. Bree had attended a few fight clubs in New Orleans but had not yet been to the one in South Texas. She wasn't even sure where it was held, but she knew it existed. Word got around.

Seamus slowly reached for the chain. He flinched when he closed his fingers around it, though the Collar did nothing. He stared at it for a long time, a swallow moving the throat the Collar would bind.

"I can't," he said in a near whisper. "I'm sorry, but I can't."

"It won't do anything but rest on your neck," Dylan assured him. "You're going to have to trust me, son. If they see you without a Collar, they'll arrest you on the spot. Or maybe they'll just shoot you."

Seamus couldn't take his eyes off the Collar. He wasn't stupid—Bree could see he fully understood that the human police would go ballistic the minute they saw Seamus with a bare neck. But the idea of wearing it was making him a little crazy. He'd never worn one, had somehow escaped the captivity that all Shifters now had to endure.

Sean contrived to look hurt. "I made that Collar meself, lad. Put me heart into it. Looks just like the real thing, doesn't it? I'm an artist."

Seamus ignored him. He snapped his gaze to Bree and held the chain out to her. "You do it."

Bree blinked. "Me? Why?"

Seamus's gaze softened. "I won't mind so much if it's your touch on my skin."

"Ah," Sean said quietly. "That's how it is, is it?"

Bree didn't answer. She noted Tiger watching them intently without seeming to—Tiger was an enigma.

Seamus had his gaze on Bree again, silent, trusting her. Bree let out a breath and took the Collar from him.

The chain was warm to the touch, where she'd expected it to be cool. The pendant had a Celtic knot in raised design on the front, a flat disk in back. Bree assumed that the pendant held the chips on the real Collars that somehow measured a change in a Shifter when he was about to get violent. Bree had no clear idea how the Collars worked—Shifters willing to discuss them believed in the theory that they had magic inside them as well as electronics.

Bree put her hand on Seamus's shoulder. His skin rippled under the shirt as he held himself back from shifting. His chest rose with a long, worried breath.

Under Bree's guiding hand, Seamus sank down to one of the kitchen chairs. The other Shifters and her mother didn't move, watching with intense scrutiny as Bree touched the chain to Seamus's neck.

He snapped his eyes closed. Bree caressed his shoulder, trying to soothe him, then she very slowly slid the Collar around his neck.

Seamus froze, the breath he'd been drawing halting in his chest. His body shuddered once, then went rigid.

Bree was about to ask Sean how the Collar clipped together in the back, when the ends joined and fused under her fingers. She blinked at the chain, which was now smooth and whole, encircling Seamus's neck, pressing into his skin, indenting it.

"It's too tight," Bree said quickly.

"The real ones are tighter, lass," Sean said. "Seamus, man, you all right?"

Seamus opened his eyes, his body stiff, his golden gaze fixing on Dylan. "You let humans put these on your family?" Rage filled his voice. "When they came for you, you surrendered and let them do *this*?" He pointed a stiff finger at the Collar. "How does that make you a good leader?"

Sean's face clouded. "Steady, lad."

Dylan said nothing. Though his expression didn't change, Bree thought she saw something uneasy inside him. The choice to take the Collar, to make his family, pride, and clan wear them, must have been painful for him.

"It was necessary," Dylan said, his tone neither admonishing nor ashamed.

"I've heard the arguments." Seamus peeled himself out of the chair, unfolding to his full height.

The Collar caught a gleam of the rising sun, glistening around his tanned throat. "That taking the Collar and living in Shiftertowns helped Shifters not starve, to have more cubs, grow stronger," he went on. "Do we look stronger right now? I have to pretend to be one of you, to bow my head and be taken away instead of fighting my way free. How does that make us stronger?"

"We can discuss it later," Dylan said, mouth tight. "You're pretending to be one of us so hell doesn't rain down on all Shifters in South Texas. When the police come in, *you* will shut up, and *I* will talk to them."

Nadine shoved her way through to the table with cups of coffee, two in each hand. She set them down, and Sean immediately grabbed one, looking relieved.

Nadine glared at Dylan. "What do you mean, *when they come in*? Police don't come into my house without a warrant. I know my rights. I'm not letting them tramp in here, getting my carpets dirty. You let *me* talk to them."

Without waiting for dissent, Nadine headed to the front, her muumuu swirling around her. She hadn't bothered to get dressed.

Bree hurried after her in alarm. Her mother didn't like police, and Bree pictured them all being arrested together and thrown into a squalid cell after Nadine gave them a piece of her mind. "Mom, wait."

"Don't worry." Nadine made it across the living room and yanked opened the front door.

The floodlights had come on, fighting with the lights from the cops' cars in the lightening grayness.

The garish glow illuminated the four uniformed police who'd climbed out of the cars and aimed handguns at the house.

"Oh, lordy," Bree said softly.

"Can I help you, officers?" Nadine stepped out onto the porch. She had a cigarette between her fingers but didn't reach for the lighter in her pocket. "Is something wrong?"

A woman in a suit with a gun in a hip holster strolled past the uniforms and toward the porch. "Ma'am, we heard word that Shifters had converged on this house. We came to see if you were all right. Are they in there?"

Bree watched her mother debate whether to lie and say the Shifters had gone or had never been there at all, versus having the police push their way in, claiming they had a right to when there was a clear danger.

Bree caught Nadine's eye, and gave her a faint nod. *Tell them the truth.*

The truth, Bree had learned, meant different things to different people.

"Yes, they're here," Nadine said. "But they're my daughter's friends. They came to breakfast."

Bree stole back into the living room and ran to the kitchen. "Make breakfast," she said rapidly to the Shifters. "I have an idea. Go with whatever I say and do."

Seamus stared at her a second or two, then he seemed to understand. He cupped her face with his big hand then let her go.

"Right," Sean said behind him. "Someone find me a mess of eggs."

***

Sean cooked. Seamus rummaged in the cupboards and removed plates and things, enough for breakfast for six. Dylan had taken up a stance at the back door, watching out the window.

Sean had eggs and bacon going in two frying pans, instructing Seamus to bring him ingredients from the refrigerator—salsa, peppers, limes, whatever Seamus could find.

Tiger was the most restless, pacing the room, checking the doors and windows as though calculating the best way out if the place was stormed.

Bree, who'd run upstairs, came barreling back down just as Seamus heard Nadine finally consent to let some of the police into her house. Bree slid into the kitchen, nearly shoved Seamus down onto a chair, and slammed herself to his lap.

She'd put on the tightest top and skirt imaginable, the skirt showing off her legs from hip to ankle. Her eyes were once more made up with eye pencil to look catlike, and she'd drawn whiskers on her face. The lines were wobbly, but solid. She'd also put on a new set of fake cat's ears.

She'd become the groupie again. Seamus couldn't decide whether she looked adorable or sexy as hell.

Bree nuzzled his neck, her arms wrapped well around him as Nadine led the police into the kitchen. Around Bree, who continued to nuzzle and kiss him, Seamus saw a woman in a suit flanked by two uniformed policemen.

The presence of the police should send him into a panic, but Seamus viewed them as though through a haze. Heat had started in his heart and was busily working its way down his body. Not only was Bree sexy as hell — okay, that was an easy decision to make — she was doing this to protect him. Mates did that.

"Bree," Nadine said in exasperation. "I told you, I don't like that groupie stuff at the table."

Bree slid from Seamus's lap, looking only slightly embarrassed as she straightened her brief skirt. "I know, but ..." She circled behind Seamus and slid her arms around him. "I can't resist him."

Not only did her clasp calm Seamus, it kept him from fingering the Collar, which was too damned tight. If he gave in to instinct and grabbed at it, he'd maybe dislodge it, revealing that it wasn't real.

Sean turned from the stove. "Breakfast is up. Dad?"

Dylan moved slowly toward the table, eyeing the police. This was a Feline used to being in charge, Seamus knew, but he'd been around long enough to know when to be forceful and when to back off. He hated backing off, Seamus saw, but a Shifter didn't get to be leader — and then keep his life after he conceded leadership — by attacking when it wasn't prudent.

Tiger underwent the biggest change. As soon as the police had entered the kitchen, he'd ceased pacing, sat down on a chair, and went still as stone. His big face was a careful blank, his yellow eyes fixed on the table.

"This is Detective Reder," Nadine said brightly. "She's worried about rogue Shifters in the area."

Reder was on the tall side for a human woman, her black hair tucked into a neat bun, her brown eyes quickly taking in the Shifters, Bree, the room, the exits, and Sean at the stove.

Seamus wondered how the detective had known they were here. He couldn't imagine Dylan and his trackers being so clumsy as to let themselves be followed, or letting them use the GPS on Bree's phone—a Guardian like Sean would have been wise enough to disable that. Or maybe it had been as simple as one of the hunters who'd been chasing him giving the police the license number of Bree's truck.

Dylan folded his arms and deliberately did not meet Reder's eyes. "These Shifters work for me. None are rogues, as you can see."

"Who are they?" Detective Reder asked crisply. "Names?"

"I'm Dylan Morrissey," Dylan answered in an even tone. "My son Sean is cooking breakfast, Tiger here is a liaison with Shifter Bureau, and Seamus McGuire is one of my trackers."

"And you are all here, because ..." The detective paused, her dark gaze impenetrable.

"Because of me," Bree said. She looked up at Reder and gave her an inane little laugh. "I couldn't let Seamus go last night—we were having *so* much fun. Dylan and the others came to find him this morning, to make sure he went back to Shiftertown like a good boy." She turned an annoyed look on Dylan and stuck her tongue out at him. "Spoilsport."

Chapter Eight

Reder transferred her interested gaze to Bree, and Bree popped her tongue back into her mouth.

Beneath her, Seamus sat rock still, his head turned so his gaze rested on Bree. Safer that way. A storm of emotions roiled in his eyes, which would betray him if he looked at Reder.

"Explain all this," Reder said to Bree. "Shifters are supposed to spend their nights in Shiftertown."

Bree kissed Seamus's cheek while she thought through what to say. The buzz of unshaved whiskers was pleasant on her lips, but she couldn't let herself get distracted.

"Seamus and me got to dancing." Bree lifted her head but gave Seamus another squeeze. "I could tell he liked me, and I asked him to come home with me." She shrugged. "We lost track of time, I guess. So his friends came looking for him."

"Trust me," Nadine said wearily. "They *did* lose track of time. But what can you do with a daughter who's addicted to Shifters?" She shook her head, the sadness of the world weighing on her shoulders.

"I'm going to need to confirm that," Reder said, still focused on Bree. "Who did you see at the roadhouse?" She didn't get out a notebook or anything, only watched Bree as though memorizing everything about her.

"Oh, lots of people." Bree screwed up her face, as though thinking then giving up. "I'm new here. I don't know everyone's names."

"But *he* would." Reder's glance fell on Seamus. "Who was there, Shifter?"

Before Seamus could speak, Sean broke in. "Me, for one. How else did I know where to start looking for the lad? Broderick, Ronan, Spike ... oh, lots of people from Shiftertown." Bree hadn't seen any of the Shifters here at the bar, but she had no doubt that Sean would make sure they all swore they'd been there.

Reder rocked on the balls of her feet. "The problem is that there's been two deaths." Her voice filled with steel. "Two men have been found dead near the roadhouse, their bodies ripped up as though by wild animals. These two men were armed, but their shotguns were likewise torn apart. No human would have been strong enough to do this, so we immediately knew ... Shifter."

Seamus stiffened. Bree rubbed her hands over his arms and pressed a kiss to his shoulder. *Keep it together,* she willed silently. *You're all right.*

Sean continued speaking for the group. "You have DNA tests now, don't you? To tell you who was at the scene? The DNA of every Shifter is on record, you know. Samples were taken way back when we were first rounded up."

Spots of red burned in Reder's cheeks. "We haven't been able to isolate the Shifter DNA yet. It's not as easy as it looks on TV."

"Ah. Maybe there's none there to isolate," Sean said.

"We'll see." Reder sounded confident. "All other evidence points to Shifter. That's why I'll have to take you all in until we discover what's going on."

Crap. At a police station, with everyone getting strip searched and the like, Seamus wouldn't be able to maintain the pretense that the Collar was real. They'd also find out Seamus wasn't from the Austin Shiftertown at all when they began going through records. Sean Morrissey might be good at verisimilitude, but Shifters couldn't work magic.

A chair scraped as Tiger climbed to his feet. Reder started and took a step back, then another as Tiger rose to his full height. The two uniformed cops swallowed, hands on weapons.

"What is he doing?" Reder asked nervously.

Tiger, in his fatigue pants and black T-shirt looked like a war-experienced soldier you did *not* want to mess with. His mixed black and orange hair went well with his hard face and unmoving golden eyes.

"Shifter Bureau," Tiger said calmly.

Reder watched him nervously. "Shifter Bureau *what*? What are you talking about?"

"Shifter Bureau must be notified if any Shifters are taken in," Tiger said. "There is a procedure. Call Major Walker Danielson, the commanding officer."

"This isn't a military thing," Reder snapped. "It's first degree murder. On *my* watch."

Tiger shook his head. "All police involvement in anything to do with Shifters must be coordinated with and cleared by Shifter Bureau."

Reder looked to Bree, of all people, for confirmation. Bree shrugged, leaning down again to rest against Seamus. It felt natural to cradle him, as though they belonged together.

Dylan broke in. "Tiger has a point. Put in a call to Shifter Bureau to confirm if you want to. You have to wait for their okay."

Reder's temper was on its last frayed thread. "To hell with Shifter Bureau. I'm arresting all Shifters in this room on suspicion of murder. I'd read you your rights, but you don't have any. You two." She pointed at Bree and Nadine. "I'll need you to stay in town, where I can put my hands on you and question you if necessary." Reder nodded at her two uniforms. "Cuff them."

The uniformed cops didn't want to do it, Bree could see, but they reluctantly took cuffs from behind their backs. None of the Shifters moved, including Seamus, who was tense as a coiled rattlesnake.

It was interesting to see that both uniformed cops tried to go for Sean first—he seemed the least threatening. Sean found it interesting too, apparently. He grinned and started backing away from them.

Reder, furious, went for Tiger.

Tiger reached out, and without changing expression, took the cuffs from Reder's hands and broke them. Reder shrieked, one of the uniforms spun around, drew his weapon, and shot Tiger.

Tiger just stood there. He didn't even look down at the red hole that blossomed in his side nor did he try to touch it.

The man who fired went sheet white. Reder drew her gun and found it plucked from her hand by Tiger's big one. Another shot rang out, this one grazing Tiger's arm, but Tiger still didn't flinch.

Tiger said, "Dylan," then his clothes were splitting, and an enormous man-beast with Tiger-striped fur filled the kitchen.

Bree expected the cops outside to come charging in, alerted by gunfire and Reder's shouts, but she saw and heard no sign of it.

The uniforms aimed again. "Stop!" Dylan's voice rang through the kitchen. "Don't provoke him. Call Shifter Bureau. Do it. *Now!*"

"I'm on it," Sean said.

"Seamus," Dylan said. "See what's happening outside."

"No one leaves this room!" Reder shouted desperately.

"I think you've been outranked, honey," Nadine said. She tapped a cigarette on the counter and put it between her lips. "Better let them find out why your backup isn't coming."

Reder snapped her fingers at one of the uniforms and grabbed the radio he handed her. "Gonzales, Smith, respond."

No answer but the crackling of static.

Bree reluctantly slid her arms from around Seamus as he got to his feet to obey Dylan. He started for the living room, but Bree went with him, because Seamus wouldn't let go of her hand.

***

They had to get out of here. Seamus's skin was roasting hot, crazy images tearing through his head, his body starting to shift of its own accord. He clamped down on the need to become lion, holding himself in human form with all his strength.

Watching Tiger taking the shots, breaking the pistol and the cuffs, and then bursting into his between beast, had surged Seamus's adrenaline high. Tiger was nearly feral, unstoppable, un-Collared, and the feral inside Seamus responded to that.

A glance out the front window showed the cops and the cars were still there. But the two uniforms were talking quietly, not looking at the house, obviously hearing nothing.

"Huh," Bree said beside him. "Maybe something is jamming the signals."

One of her fake cat's ears brushed Seamus's arm. A deep shiver went through him, a need so strong he knew he'd not contain it for long.

Bree had no idea how good she looked in the skirt that hugged her ample curves, the makeup she'd already smeared, even the silly cat's ears. Seamus wondered why every male in the roadhouse last night hadn't tried to carry her off.

The thought made him rumble with growls. Even the briefest image of another Shifter touching her had Seamus's anger soaring.

To hell with Dylan and his tame Shifters, to hell with the human cops and the hunters. Seamus needed Bree — didn't want to be without her, ever again. Anything else going on in this house right now was irrelevant.

Seamus grasped her arm. "Come with me," he said, his voice barely working.

Bree's blue eyes behind the black paint widened. "Come with you where?"

"Out of here. Away. We'll go far from here, hole up, stay together."

Bree's mouth formed a round *O*. Seamus expected her to look terrified, to yank herself from him, to fight him with the courage he'd seen in her.

No fear filled her eyes. Instead, Seamus saw interest, curiosity, and longing.

Then Bree's face fell. "I can't. I can't leave my mom to deal with Shifters and the cops by herself."

No, she couldn't. Bree's family might be very small, but Seamus had seen the fierce loyalty between mother and daughter, the shared grief over the brother, the way they took care of each other.

"Bring her," Seamus said. "I'll protect her too. But I have to go, now that I'm healed. I have no choice."

Bree's mouth dropped open again. "Wait, you want me to run away with you and 'hole up,' as you said ... *with my mother?*"

"We will take care of her. It's the Shifter way."

"The Shifter way is the crazy way." Bree's smile held incredulity. "Anyway, it doesn't matter. We'll never get out past the cops."

"I can."

"Yeah, I bet *you* can." Bree looked him up and down. "But I can't."

"I'll work on it. Bree ..." Seamus couldn't help touching her, skimming her hair back from her face. The headband snagged on his fingers. "There's so much I need to tell you. But I have to get away from here, *now*, can't be arrested. It's important."

Bree's expression was serious. "Did you really kill the hunters?"

Confused memories beat into his brain. The blood, the pain, snarling, screams, the smell ... "I don't know. It's ... unclear." Seamus took Bree's hand again, pressing down. "Now that I've found you, I can't let you go. I *can't*. I never would have healed this fast if not for you."

"You said that last night. But if you needed to leave so bad, why didn't you go? I mean, this morning before we woke up? Before the Shifters came. If you'd gone in the night, they might not have found you."

Seamus was already shaking his head. "Because I didn't want to leave without you. I wanted to convince you to come with me." Humor trickled through his frustration. "I was stupid. Which is also down to you — my brains went out the window when I landed in your truck and laid eyes on you. There's things I have to do. I have to know they're safe — Goddess, please let them be safe — but I'm running out of time." His words tumbled out, his worry escalating.

"If you really need to leave," Bree said. "I can distract them. You're Shifter — I'm pretty sure you can be gone faster than they can think to start looking for you."

Seamus pulled his attention back to what she was saying. Offering to stay behind, to take the wrath of the police so Seamus could slip out and go. Sacrifice.

Did Seamus have a choice? Either way, he lost. If he left without Bree, he'd likely never see her again. If he stayed, he'd fail his mission and those who counted on him. *Can't have both.*

What the human cops and Shifter Bureau didn't understand was that Shifters were more than animals. Eons ago, when Shifters had been created as fighters for the Fae, those Shifters were more primal. If he'd lived back then, Seamus might have said to hell with his responsibilities and Bree's family, grabbed her, and headed off. They'd go somewhere remote, lose themselves, never return.

But since then Shifters had learned about communities. Didn't matter about Collars, no Collars, or what species each Shifter was — another thing humans, and even the Collared Shifters, didn't always understand. Seamus could be as protective of those in his community — the Lupines, bears, and Felines not remotely related to him — as he was with his own family.

Who were all gone. Kendrick's band of Shifters had been made up of those left on their own. Kendrick had known how to draw them together so they formed one big clan, no matter what their origins.

Now the clan had dissipated, each Shifter having his or her designated responsibilities to carry out before they reunited. Kendrick seemed to have vanished off the face of the earth for now, but it didn't matter. He'd be back. He always came back.

Come away with me. Seamus wanted that more than anything. For Bree to become part of his family, part of his pride.

Seamus opened his mouth to tell Bree he had a better idea when a huge noise sounded behind the attic ceiling in the stairwell above them.

With a rush and a roar, the plaster and boards of the ceiling came down, along with a deluge of water, the entirety of it crashing into the stairs and the floor below.

Chapter Nine

Bree screamed. Dust, boards, sheetrock, and water poured down the stairs, and Seamus slammed himself over Bree, feeling debris pound his back. He smelled dirt, water, blood.

Tiger was the first one out of the kitchen. He was a full tiger now, giant paws sending up plumes of water as he bounded across the flooded living room, shoving aside wood and pieces of wallboard to get to them. Once they were free, Tiger stood over them, staring down with intense yellow eyes.

Bree was coughing, but unhurt. Seamus felt a sting on his face and wiped away blood, but it was only from cuts from the exploding pieces of wallboard and plaster.

"We're all right," Seamus said.

Tiger turned from them and leapt up the stairs. Dylan and Sean had emerged after Tiger and had already started for the attic. Reder was close on their heels, slipping on the now soaked rugs and floorboards. One of the uniforms followed, his weapon drawn, Nadine coming behind. What had happened to the second uniform cop was unclear.

"You won't want to go up there." Nadine called after them as Reder and the cop headed upstairs. "It's dangerous."

"Whoever is up there is coming down," Detective Reder declared.

"It's my son," Nadine said. She'd stopped at the foot of the stairs, resting her hands on the newel post.

Reder glared down at her. "Then you tell him to come out quietly."

"Can't. He's passed. Killed in action. I mean it's his ghost. He's watching over us."

Reder's face was a mixture of sympathy and anger. "I'm sorry to hear about your son, ma'am. But whoever is up there is no ghost."

She turned away leaving Seamus, Bree, and Nadine alone.

"Mom." Bree signaled her mother over and spoke in a rapid whisper. "We need to go. Me and Seamus. He has things he has to do."

Seamus brushed debris from his shirt. "Bree doesn't want to leave you behind. Come with us."

Nadine looked him over in surprise, then she gave a snort, her short curls bouncing. "Like I'm going to go running through empty lots or hiding in the back of Remy's pickup. You do what you need to, *but*—" She stuck two fingers against Seamus's chest. "You look after my daughter. Bring her home in one piece. You got me? I know you didn't kill those men, so you prove it. Now go." Nadine glanced at the ceiling and smiled. "You know why their radios are jammed? It's Remy, messing with the signals. That was his job in the army, remember?"

She turned and started up the stairs. Above, the Shifters were scrambling into the attic, Reder demanding to know what they saw.

Seamus took Bree's hand, led her through the kitchen, and out the back door.

***

Bree already knew that going for the pickup would be impossible. Remy's truck was parked in front and currently surrounded by cops. The uniform who hadn't come out of the kitchen was out there with the other two, explaining what was going on.

Bree had grabbed her purse from the kitchen counter as they'd sped out, and now she tucked the bulky thing under her arm. "Well, you wanted a distraction," she said to Seamus. "This way."

She led him out of their small yard and across a field to a strand of live oaks growing thickly along a creek. The creek was low, only a trickle in it, but the damp bed and the trees gave them cover. Bree was glad she hadn't put on spike heels to complete her groupie costume. She'd grabbed plain flats instead, needing to hurry through the house.

She worried about leaving her mother behind, but one thing Bree knew about Nadine Fayette was that she could hold her own. She'd raised two kids by herself after their dad died, had dealt with a hell of a lot of stuff. A Shifter like Dylan might be powerful, but Bree doubted he'd had to deal with anyone like her mother.

After they'd hiked about half a mile, Bree in the lead, she said, "All right, Seamus. We have a little time as we run for our lives. Tell me what this is all about. You said you didn't know if you killed the hunters. How could you not know?"

Seamus didn't speak for a moment and was so quiet Bree feared he'd slipped away and left her. She quickly turned around, but he was a step behind her, sunlight touching his dark hair and glittering in his eyes.

"Everything is a blur," he said, his voice a low growl. "I was being chased, I thought by the hunters. But when someone attacked me, I thought it was Shifter, and I didn't hold back. I couldn't see clearly, and scent was one mass of confusion. I never would have killed humans like that. I could only have done that if I'd gone feral."

"Or you really were fighting a Shifter, and he killed the hunters."

"I've considered that too." Seamus let out a heavy sigh. "But I don't remember." His voice went even more growling, as though he longed to shift into his animal form. "Things were flicking in and out all night. I changed safe houses, because I swore we were being stalked. I went back to the first safe house to ambush the attacker, to draw him to follow *me*. Everything after that ... I can't be sure. Until I saw the hunters were dead, and I ran, getting shot along the way. I saw you sitting in your truck and headed for it."

"And then what?" Bree jumped a small trickle of water, grateful for Seamus steadying her on the muddy bank. "Everything suddenly cleared up?"

"No." Seamus gave a short laugh. "I was being chased by hunters and in the car with a crazy woman."

"Not crazy ... well, not *much* crazy."

"I was half passed out with pain," Seamus said. "But everything since I met you, I remember. I haven't faded out again."

"That's good. Where is this safe house? Is that where we're going?"

"Only if we can make sure we aren't followed." Seamus paused to push a branch out of her way. It was quiet back here, and humid, Bree's hair already damp. "I have to get there, check on it, but I can't risk leading anyone there. It's very important."

"I'll make sure," Bree said. "I didn't exactly have an angelic childhood."

Seamus didn't respond to that, and Bree glanced behind her. Seamus was following closely, and again, he put out a hand to help her keep her balance.

"So what do you think happened in my attic?" she asked as they trudged along. "Water pipe bursting? A leak would explain the shorting light you saw."

"I don't know." Seamus sounded troubled. "I didn't like the smell."

"Yeah? I have a feeling you don't mean like an animal that crawled in there and died."

"No, it was sharper," Seamus said. "A scent no Shifter wants to smell in his lifetime. If your house is on a ley line, it could be a gate into the Fae lands. The scent wasn't strong, so the opening might be weak. But if your house *is* on a ley line, I want you to move."

"Oh, right. I don't think my mom will go for that. The house is paid for." Bree navigated over a boulder, clinging to Seamus's strong hand. "I've heard Shifters talk about the Fae. They *made* you a long time ago, right? And now you hate them?"

"Shifters have always hated Fae. It's nothing new."

Seamus pulled her to a halt. Standing with him, Bree felt right, no matter that they were hurrying through a creek bed evading cops and Shifters with Collars or whoever. She belonged here, leaning against him.

"I don't hear anyone following," Seamus said. "We need to stop and think. Where are you trying to take me?"

Bree shrugged, liking the warmth of his shirt against her shoulder. "To find a car, one that won't be missed for a while." One that wouldn't land on a police report until they were long gone. "Remy taught me how to hotwire."

"You miss him," Seamus said.

"Yeah." Bree blinked suddenly moist eyes. "I do. He always had time for his pesky little sister. Losing him put a big hole in my life, you know?"

Seamus drew his hand down her back. "I do know. I lost my brother and sister, my mom. It was before Shifters were rounded up. When they started coming after Shifters, planning to shut them in Shiftertowns, I ran and hid out. I ran to a lot of places before I found some Shifters to stay with. I'd been alone a long time, but I'm not anymore. They took me in."

Seamus closed his mouth to a thin line as though he wanted to say more but stopped himself.

One day, Bree vowed, she'd make him tell her the entire story. Right now, though, they couldn't stay down in this creek bed forever.

"This way," she said, pointing down a side trail. "It will take us to a more populated area, where we can find an old car."

Seamus pressed a kiss to the top of her head. "How do you know your way around here? I thought humans stuck to sidewalks."

Bree gave him a laugh. "I grew up in the bayous. Learned to explore the backwoods when I was tiny. When I moved here, the first thing I did was figure out where all these little paths out here went. Easier than the bayous, trust me. There are plenty of snakes in this part of Texas, but no alligators. That's a plus."

Seamus didn't laugh, only listened as though she imparted important information. He gave her another kiss on the head, then pulled away as though worried he wouldn't let go if he didn't make himself.

While Bree was not happy they had to walk on, putting distance between themselves and her house, she knew now was not the time and place to indulge in her growing desires for Seamus. In movies, people stopped and had sex in the middle of running away or fighting, but that was the movies. This was real life, and dangerous.

Bree headed down an overgrown path, the two of them ducking under low-hanging branches. About half a mile later, they emerged in a weed-choked ditch that was bridged over for the road above it.

They were on the southwestern outskirts of Austin, which had built up so much in the last ten years, people had told Bree, that it was running into the towns around it. Bree, new to the area, only saw strip malls, housing developments, restaurants, and giant hardware stores.

At the end of a string of stores selling farm equipment, building equipment, and lumber, Bree found cars sitting empty and forlorn in a parking lot. The dirt on them and the ground around them told her they'd been there for some time. Possibly because they didn't work, or maybe the owners just didn't know how to haul them off.

Only one way to find out. Bree went to the most whole-looking of them and opened the unlocked door.

Seamus crouched down next to her as Bree pried open the panel under the steering wheel and tugged out the wiring. Old cars were easier to hotwire than new ones, which were computerized and might have failsafes to keep the car from working if the steering column was broken. A pro car thief could get around it; an amateur like Bree could not.

This car was old enough for their needs. Bree's hands grew moist, her fingers shaking as she strove to remember what wires Remy had taught her to touch together.

There. A spark jumped from wire to wire. The car sputtered to life, and then died. Bree tapped the

wires again, getting sparks, but the engine didn't
make a sound.

"Damn it."

Seamus said nothing, only rose and helped her
up. The next one Bree tried had the same result. The
blasted things had been here too long.

Seamus, who could have been yelling at her to
hurry or berating her for not being able to do what
she claimed she could, only patiently escorted her to
the next car. No one else was in the lot, though the
sun was well up now; no one seemed to spot them
flitting from vehicle to vehicle.

The fourth car Bree tried finally struggled to life.
She revved the engine, rewarded by a steady hum,
not gurgling death throes. She let out her breath.
"Finally."

The tank was almost empty, and Bree would have
to fill it. She was grateful she'd had sense enough to
bring her purse, which held a little bit of cash. Credit
cards or bank cards would be off limits — those were
easily traced. Good thing there were enough people
in Texas — as had been in the bayous — who didn't
trust credit cards and banks, so Bree making cash
purchases wouldn't be regarded as unusual and
memorable.

First, to get there.

"All right," Bree said as Seamus slid into the
passenger seat. "We have transportation. Where are
we going?"

"North," Seamus said.

"Can you be more specific?" Bree put the car in
gear and carefully drove out of the lot. No one
yelled, no one came running, no one seemed to
notice.

Bree glanced at Seamus, sitting so casually next to her as he had in her truck last night, but washed and nearly recovered this morning. He was watching the surrounding area and other cars, sun glinting on the fake Collar resting against his throat.

"I'm not sure from here," he answered after a time. "Go north, toward the city."

Bree wasn't as familiar with this area as she wanted to be, but she picked a large, high-trafficked road and turned the direction she thought was north. A green sign with "Austin" on it plus an arrow pointing the way didn't hurt.

"Of all the Shifters in all the world who could jump into my truck," Bree muttered, "I got one who's directionally challenged."

Seamus slanted her a look from his golden eyes. "And I got a Shifter groupie with smeared makeup." He ran a gentle finger down her cheek.

Bree went hot. "Smeared because I was saving your ass."

"I know. By showing off *your* sweet ass."

Bree went hotter still. "Oh, you like it, do you?"

"Yes. And what you felt like under your sleep shirt, when I kissed you last night." He skimmed his touch to her shoulder. "I liked it."

"Yeah?" Bree softened her banter. "Well, so did I."

"Good." Seamus looked around again, but she saw the flush on his face, the need in his eyes. "I remember this now. Take that road."

That road was Mopac, which led right through the heart of Austin. Seamus was searching, searching as they sped up the highway—and then slowed down for a ton of traffic. It was eight in the morning, and Mopac was clogged.

Seamus kept quiet until they'd crossed the river. Then he came alert, pointing to a sign they were fast approaching. "Enfield, that was it."

Bree pulled hurriedly across two lanes, earning honks, yells, and fingers, diving for the exit. Seamus directed her east, and they drove on again. Enfield was a quieter, if narrow street, heading up a hill before it descended again toward the tall buildings of downtown.

Seamus was peering carefully around again, directing her down a side street and then to another little artery that seemed to go nowhere.

"You know, we're almost out of gas," Bree pointed out.

"Not far now," Seamus said absently.

They ended up at Lamar. Seamus directed her south on this street, then into a smaller neighborhood. The houses here were nearly obscured with overgrown trees and bushes. Old houses perched on rises above the street, stone stairs leading up to them.

"Are you sure this is right?" Bree asked. "This is like the middle of downtown Austin. Well, very close, anyway. You know, with police stations and everything."

"I know," Seamus said. "Here." He pointed.

Bree guided the old car to the curb, or rather, the side of the road. There were no sidewalks, just the narrow street hidden among trees and behind a curve of hill that followed the Colorado River. Bree knew that they were in the middle of the city—with people in cars rushing everywhere—but in this little area, hidden from all eyes, they might have been in the quiet countryside.

"Not what I expected," Bree said in a hushed voice.

Seamus climbed out of the car and carefully shut its door—no slamming. Bree joined him, taking the same amount of care.

Seamus gave her a half smile as he waited for her. "Did you think I'd bring you to a burned-out shack in the middle of nowhere? Even rogue Shifters like running water and electricity."

"Funny." Bree wrinkled her nose. "Lead on."

Seamus took her to a flight of steps that went up the hill, each individual step nestled into the earth. They climbed about fifteen of these, trees closing around them to shield them from passers-by on the road. Not that Bree saw or heard anyone.

Seamus pulled off his fake Collar as they walked, the ends unfusing at his touch as easily as they'd joined. Bree wondered how on earth Sean had made it to do that. He truly was an artist.

At the end of the steps lay a narrow dirt path, at the end of the path a house. The house was small, white, and needing paint, with a wide porch of the bungalow style. The windows were framed by black shutters, also needing paint. The yard around it had seen better days, the grass yellow now with coming winter. At one time, though, Bree could tell, flower beds had lined the path and the perimeter of the house. The whole place was quaint, tiny, and the kind of place Bree would love to live.

Seamus walked up to the front porch, took a key from his pocket at the same time he stuffed the Collar into it, and unlocked and opened the door. He entered the house first to make sure all was well within, as Shifters did.

"All right, Francesca?" he called softly inside.

Francesca? Who the hell was ...

Must be the tall woman with a mass of brown hair coming down the stairs, her rangy look telling Bree she was Lupine.

The Shifter who came galloping from the back at the sound of Seamus's voice wasn't Lupine—or Feline either. It was a bear, a brown one, and very, very small. He, or she, barreled toward Seamus on short legs with oversized paws, and ran smack into him.

Chapter Ten

Seamus rocked a little as the cub slammed into his legs, then he paused to let himself feel vast relief. Katie was all right.

Bree, behind him, stopped in astonishment. Seamus felt the waves of her confusion and wonder roll off her.

"And who is *this*?" Bree asked with eager interest.

The little bear was clinging to Seamus's leg, claws coming through his jeans, as Bree's cat's had done this morning.

"This is Katie," Seamus said, his voice a low rumble. "I'm looking after her."

Katie looked up at her name. The cub was about two years old in human terms, which was barely born in Shifter. She needed constant care.

"But what is she doing here?" Bree asked, amazed. "She's Shifter, right? What happened to her parents? Or are you ...?" She broke off, looking at Francesca. Cross species mating did happen.

Francesca unbent enough to bark a laugh. "Not mine. Seamus found her."

"Found her?" Bree swung her focus to Seamus.

"More or less," Seamus said.

He didn't want to describe how he'd come across Katie's bear Shifter mother, dead from bringing Katie in. He'd found them all alone in the wilds in northern Manitoba, near Hudson Bay. Katie's mother had been Collared—all Seamus could figure was that she had escaped her Shiftertown for whatever reason to have her child alone.

Seamus had fetched Kendrick, who'd sent the mother to dust with his Sword of the Guardian then taken the cub to foster with others. Kendrick's Shifters had many foster cubs, rescued from similar situations. The cubs were split up among the Shifters who had the ability to take care of them.

Seamus wasn't fostering Katie—Francesca was. When Kendrick's compound had been raided and destroyed, the protocol was that certain trackers were put in charge of making sure cubs and their mothers, natural and foster, were taken care of. Seamus was one of those trackers, his assignment, Katie and Francesca.

"Any trouble?" Seamus asked.

Francesca shook her head. "Not a peep. Katie's getting restless, though. She wants to run."

Bree crouched down, and Katie gamboled over to her. She sniffed Bree over, while Bree watched, enraptured, then Bree put out a tentative hand to pet her. Katie gave a baby growl and rubbed her head against Bree's hand.

Then Katie reached up one paw and plucked the cat's ears, forgotten by Bree, from her head. The cub adjusted the headband on her own head with great dexterity, then returned to four paws and started loping around the room. Bree sat back, a stunned look on her face.

"If you take her out running in Zilker Park, people will notice," she said, her voice faint. "You'll be inundated with questions. And possibly arrested."

Francesca broke in. "All right, Seamus, who *is* this woman, and why did you bring a human to a safe house?"

Seamus returned Francesca's look with a calm one. "This is Bree Fayette. She saved my life last night. Bree, Francesca."

"Mmm." Francesca didn't look happy, but she gave Bree a nod. "Now that she knows about us, you know you can't let her go."

"I won't keep her prisoner," Seamus said. Francesca, unfortunately was one of those all-or-nothing Shifters. Shifters should keep to themselves, no humans trusted, unless they were brought in and confined.

Bree gave Francesca a look of annoyance with her cat-outlined eyes. "Seriously? I helped pick bullets out of him and got him away from a bunch of cops— you really think I'll rat you out now?"

"You're one of those groupies," Francesca said, her nostrils pinching.

"Which means I like Shifters and want what's best for them," Bree returned. She looked up at Seamus from the floor. "You sure we're safe here?"

"Pretty sure," Seamus said. "As soon as I ditch the car."

Bree's eyes widened. "Leaving us with no transportation?"

"We won't need it," Seamus said. "We'll lie low here for a while." Until Kendrick contacted them. Those were the orders.

"*I'll* ditch it," Francesca said. "Keys?"

"No keys," Bree said. "It's wired. I should do it."

"I can deal with that." Francesca was already on her way out the door. "I'll hide it somewhere we can get to it if we need it again."

The screen door banged. Katie stopped her running and looked out the screen after Francesca, then came to Bree and climbed decidedly onto her lap. Bree closed her arms around bear fur, and Katie leaned into her.

"Poor little thing," Bree said. "Francesca seems ... intense. Are you sure you trust *her*?"

Seamus folded himself down next to them. "She's a tracker. Our Shifter leader believes females are as good at tracking as males. Francesca is naturally suspicious of any outsider, with good reason." He let out his breath. "Bree, I don't know what the hell is going to happen. It's always been so simple before."

Bree scratched the top of Katie's head. "Why is it complicated now?"

"Because of you." Seamus gave her an open look. "I don't know how much I can risk telling you. I don't know if things will play out for my Shifters like they did before. I don't know if I'm going feral or if it's a temporary thing. I don't know if I killed those hunters. I don't know if I'll have to disappear and never see you again." He touched Bree's hair. "That's killing me most of all."

***

Bree stared up at him, lips parted. Her entire body squeezed into one tight, painful point. Embracing the bear cub sent a warm, soothing trickle through her, but Seamus's declaration had her heart aching.

His eyes, intent on her, were golden and warm, his touch electric. Here they were, sitting in a rundown house in the middle of town, stranded in this island of calm—with a bear cub and a Lupine woman who'd come back inside any time. And Bree knew right then she was falling in love with a Shifter.

She barely knew him, and after Seamus got himself and Katie safe, she might never see him again. This could be one of those encounters she'd remember the rest of her life, something to relive in the middle of a lonely night. The great love that wasn't meant to be.

Katie, restless again, slid out of Bree's lap and waddled away, the cat's ears still on her head. She sat down on her bottom, took them off, and studied them every which way. Then she curled up around them and closed her eyes. In a few moments, she emitted a baby snore.

Seamus came down to Bree, folding his body around her, arms cradling her. His lips brushed Bree's neck, moving up under her ear, his breath hot. Bree turned her head and caught his mouth with hers.

The kiss began slowly, a savoring, a learning. Seamus smelled of the wet green stream they'd run along, sweat, himself. He cupped her neck in his strong hand, his lips parting hers, the kiss deepening.

The corners of Bree's heart, empty and sad, began to fill. The warmth inside her changed to heat that flared and started to consume her.

She wound her hand behind Seamus's neck, pulling him closer. Seamus came readily, his arms enfolding her, his mouth a fine place.

They kissed without frenzy, desire a leisurely burn between them. The few days' growth of Seamus's whiskers scraped Bree's lips, his mouth intoxicating. Seamus spread his hand on the back of her neck, cradling her into him. His chest was hard under Bree's touch, his heart beating rapidly. Arms and legs around her held her securely, his body shielding her from the world.

The door banged open and Francesca strode back inside. Bree expected Seamus to jump away, but he didn't. He kept his arms around Bree, slowly finishing the kiss before he raised his head.

Katie didn't wake. The cub seemed to understand that she was safe with Seamus here, her sides rising and falling in deep, even breaths.

Francesca paused in the doorway, her sharp gaze taking in Seamus and Bree on the floor. Seamus kept his arm around Bree as though it was the most natural thing in the world.

Francesca let the door close. "Your timing sucks, Seamus," she said.

Seamus moved one shoulder in a shrug. "Things happen when they happen."

"How much does she know?" Francesca asked.

"*She* is sitting right here," Bree said. "I know you're hiding out from the entire world, because you're un-Collared and I'm guessing you want to stay that way. *How* you are, I haven't figured out. I don't think you pulled your Collars off." Like Seamus, Francesca had no red line around her neck to indicate she'd ripped a Collar out of her skin. The small indentation the fake Collar had left on Seamus was nothing to what a real Collar would have done.

Francesca scowled, her Lupine gray eyes fiery. "You don't need to know that."

"Doesn't matter," Bree said. "You're stuck here, and you have to take care of Katie. What's going to happen when you need food? You'll drive a stolen car to the grocery store down the street? Not every human recognizes Shifters, but you both will stand out. You have a *look*."

Even more than most Collared Shifters Bree had known, even more than the Shifters she'd met this morning, Francesca and Seamus had a wildness about them that other Shifters lacked.

"Well, we have *you* now," Francesca said to her. "You can shop for us."

"Right," Bree countered. "I just sneaked a Shifter away from a bunch of cops. They probably put out an APB on me. Every store clerk will be on the lookout, hoping for a reward."

"Enough." Seamus's one growled word didn't have to be loud. He rose to his feet—straight up from a sitting position, no scrambling. Francesca snapped her mouth closed, though her eyes showed her fury.

"Bree is one of us, not a hostage. She saved my life—twice. I owe her."

Francesca growled. "I saw you giving her a little payback."

A lion snarl came from Seamus's throat. He took one step toward Francesca, who danced a few paces back on quick feet.

Francesca wasn't as dominant as Seamus, Bree realized, watching them. She'd seen enough dominance skirmishes at the Shifter bars in New Orleans to understand what was going on here.

But Francesca wasn't less dominant simply because she was female. Plenty of females were higher than males in the hierarchy. She was simply not *as* high as Seamus. She was testing him, maybe trying to see if he'd muscle her into obedience over Bree.

From Seamus's soft growls, he was going to protect Bree. Francesca saw that and started backing off, her shoulders rounding, her head drooping as she conceded.

Seamus went to Francesca, stood silently in front of her for a few seconds, then pulled her into an embrace. Not a sensual one, not like the tender way Seamus had held Bree. This was reassurance, like a father giving his cub a lick.

Seamus didn't exactly lick Francesca, but he pressed her into the hug, holding her tight. Francesca's arms came around him, hugging him back, the tension going out of her.

When he released her, he touched her shoulder, then returned to Bree. Dominance reestablished, Seamus was showing Francesca he'd take care of her. All was well.

Through it all, Katie slept. The bear cub was boneless on the carpet, her small snores both adorable and comforting. Complete trust.

Francesca came to Bree, and when she spoke, her tone was much more respectful. "Katie likes you," Francesca said. "She doesn't take to everyone."

"Is it hard to look after a bear?" Bree asked in true curiosity. "Being a wolf?"

"Hell, yeah," Francesca said. "In the wild, I'd never have dreamed it. But Katie is just so ... well, cute."

Francesca still wasn't happy with Seamus bringing Bree here, Bree could see, but Francesca said nothing more about it. Bree had some sympathy—for all Francesca knew, Bree was some kind of undercover spy for Shifter Bureau, who would worm their secrets out of them and turn them in. Bureau police would come out with nets and tranq guns and round up Seamus, Francesca, and Katie to stuff them into cages and decide what to do with them.

"I know you don't trust me," Bree said. "But really, I'm not from Shifter Bureau or anything like that—I don't even know where their offices are. I'm Bree Fayette, from a town in Louisiana you've never heard of, I moved out here with my mom when we inherited a house from my great-uncle, and there wasn't anything left for us at home. I'm a Shifter groupie, of a sort. I love Shifters and everything about them. I'd never hurt you, or help anyone hurt you, no matter how bitchy you get, and I'd certainly never do anything to harm a cub like Katie. You don't have to believe me, but that's the naked truth."

Francesca listened, brows rising. Seamus wasn't exactly smiling, but his eyes were full of warmth.

"Yeah, well," Francesca said. "Don't say *naked*. Seamus might go into mating frenzy with you right here on the carpet, and I so don't need to see that."

***

Katie slept on. At Seamus's suggestion, Bree carried her into an upstairs bedroom and lay down with her. Francesca let them go, saying nothing.

Seamus knew Francesca had snarled at him to see how far he'd let her go, to discover what Bree was to him. He'd told her, all right.

Francesca had watched with cautious eyes as Seamus escorted Bree and Katie upstairs, but didn't try to interfere. She was trusting him.

Seamus kissed Bree briefly on the lips after she settled on the bed with Katie. He pulled a blanket over Bree and went out into the upstairs hall, where a window let him keep watch on the front perimeter. Francesca prowled restlessly downstairs.

Now to settle in and wait for Kendrick.

Seamus had no doubt his leader would be in touch, telling them where to regroup—it was just a matter of time. This was the toughest part of all, though, the waiting. Seamus had been trained to sit tight and wait for orders, but that time could be brutal.

When Kendrick finally revealed where his Shifters would meet again, Seamus would ask Bree to come with him. He was pretty sure she'd say no, because accompanying him would mean going into hiding with him somewhere in the world, leaving her mother and everything she knew behind. Bree would have to make that choice, and there was no reason she would choose him. Seamus would lose her, when he'd only just found her.

That thought hurt. Waiting here in this house was going to be hard—leaving would be harder.

The day wore on. Bree and Katie slept soundly. Francesca ceased her prowling and took a nap, leaving Seamus to stand guard.

At about five in the afternoon, Seamus saw movement in the shadows under the trees that lined the front yard.

He stiffened as the shadow slipped from the trees around to the side of the house. Seamus ran silently down the stairs, imagining the path the intruder must have taken. He got himself behind the back door just as a floorboard on the porch creaked. The intruder took one step, then two, then reached the door.

Seamus flung it open, grabbed the Shifter on the other side of it, and hauled him inside. It was a Lupine, the one he'd seen at Bree's house this morning—Broderick.

Just as Seamus registered that fact, the lock on the front door broke without fanfare, and the door banged open. The Bengal tiger Shifter walked inside.

"Bree is here," Tiger announced in his slow voice. "And a cub."

Chapter Eleven

Francesca came off the sofa, snarling, and attacked Tiger. Tiger turned his head, put out one massive arm, and shoved. Francesca soared straight back through the air, landing heavily on the sofa, and started to shift.

Seamus got between her and Tiger. *"Stop!"* he commanded.

Francesca's eyes narrowed. "We can take him," she said, her voice clogged with the change. "He's Collared."

Broderick answered from the kitchen doorway. "Not really. Tiger's kind of ... special."

Tiger gave Broderick a flat yellow stare, then Francesca, then Seamus. Francesca drew a breath, dropped back to the sofa, and stayed human. "What the hell is he?" she asked Seamus.

"We're not sure," Broderick said before Seamus could speak. "Okay, *I'm* not sure. His mate thinks he's all sweet and cuddly, but Carly's about to bring in his cub, so she's gushy right now. The rest of us know he's just crazy." Broderick's sharp gaze went to Seamus. The Lupine might seem nonchalant and a smartass, but he wasn't stupid. "Where's Bree?"

"Here." Bree stood on the stairs. "What do you want?"

Seamus growled. "I know what they want. How did you find us?" he asked Broderick. "No way you tracked us."

Broderick shrugged. "No way *most* Shifters could have tracked you. You went to ground fast and pretty good. But there are trackers, and then there's Tiger."

Tiger stood quietly, offering no explanation. "There is a cub here."

"Seamus, who the hell are they?" Francesca demanded, scared. She was afraid for Katie, terrified the cub would be taken. Her mission, and Seamus's, was to keep the cubs free. Tiger should not have known Katie was here. Seamus hadn't betrayed her existence with word or deed. He hadn't even told Bree, as much as he'd been tempted to trust her, until he'd brought her here.

Broderick hadn't known—he looked surprised. "Tiger just seems to know where cubs are and when they're in trouble. He has this this search-and-rescue thing going on."

Tiger started for the stairs. Seamus grabbed for him to stop him, but found himself holding empty air.

Bree got in front of Tiger and blocked the way up the stairs. "You leave her alone!"

Seamus went for Tiger again, landing on the bigger man's back. He remembered the cops shooting Tiger at the house, and Tiger just staring at them. Seamus knew it was a mean thing to do, but he jabbed his hand where he remembered the bullet wound had been.

Tiger snarled. He swung around—fast—then rapidly became a tiger, his clothes splitting and falling away. Francesca came off the sofa again and tried to tackle him. Seamus ended up on top of her as Tiger threw them both off.

Bree was yelling. Tiger simply bumped her out of the way as he flowed up the stairs. Bree grabbed his tail as he passed, but Tiger kept going, pulling Bree along with him.

Seamus was up and after them, Francesca right behind him. Broderick leisurely brought up the rear. "She's got Tiger by the tail," he said. "Not a great place to be."

Seamus reached the second floor to see Tiger moving unerringly into the bedroom where they'd left Katie, Bree clinging grimly on to his tail.

Seamus made it to the door. Inside, Katie was standing up on the bed, her bear eyes wide. When the enormous tiger stopped at the bedside, Katie reached out and put one paw on his nose.

Tiger rumbled low in his throat. He closed his eyes and let Katie sniff him then give his huge face an inquisitive lick. Bree let go of Tiger's tail, staying very still as she watched.

Seamus held his breath. He felt no distress at all from Katie. Curiosity, wonder, trust. Amazement that Tiger was so big, but no worries at all.

Tiger sank down on his belly with a huff of breath. He was so big that, lying down, his back was in line with the top of the mattress. Katie kept sniffing him, then she climbed on his back, clinging with her little bear claws, and rested her chin on top of his head. Tiger huffed again and settled down, doing nothing that would disturb Katie.

"See what I mean?" Broderick said behind them. "The cubs, they love him. It's some program, or some genetic whatever-the-hell-they-did-to-his-head kind of shit in the lab where they raised him. Anyway, let me cut to the chase." He leaned his big Lupine body against the door, tatts moving on his upper arms as he folded them. "Tiger was sent to track you down, me to talk—Tiger sometimes talks and sometimes doesn't. Dylan wants you to come in. To Shiftertown, I mean. We'll fix you up with fake Collars, and Sean will put you in the database so it will look like you've always been there. He's probably already done it. You stop running, the cub is safe."

Francesca growled at him, glaring with gray wolf eyes, testing his dominance. Broderick returned her look without concern. Seamus could tell Broderick was pretty high in the dominance chain himself, about level with Seamus. Not as high as Sean Morrissey, definitely not in the same class as Dylan.

"Like hell I'm taking Katie to a Shiftertown," Francesca snarled. "She's only two years old. I'm not letting you put a Collar on her—ever. She's not living in captivity. She's a wild bear, and she's staying that way."

Anger flashed in Broderick's eyes—a Shifter who didn't like backtalk. Well, he'd always get it from Francesca. She'd acknowledge her place in the hierarchy, but if she thought someone above her was an asshole, she'd say so.

"You think I'd stick a real Collar on a baby?" Broderick asked, voice harsh. "No Collars for cubs. Dylan and Liam won't let it happen. She'll get a fake when she's around five or six, to keep the humans fooled. You and Seamus here will have to wear fakes too. We can't let on that you've never been Collared."

"How about this?" Seamus countered, his calmer voice a contrast to Francesca's fierce one. "You give us a ride somewhere far from here, where Katie will be safe. Then turn around and leave us alone. We have things to do."

He felt Bree watching him. Now was the time for choice. Would Bree come with him if he asked? Or refuse? And then what would Seamus do? Run with Francesca and keep Katie protected, or stay with Bree, who was bonding with his heart?

He couldn't leave Katie, a helpless cub, but taking Bree with them would put her in danger as well. Bree also had a life, a mom, friends, a home. She'd be secure and happy in her normal existence—as long as she stayed away from Shifters.

Katie isn't yours, a voice in his head whispered. *She's not even a Feline. You have no reason to take care of her. Bree is your mate. Grab her and don't let her go.*

If Seamus listened to the voices, he'd truly go feral.

Katie made a small, happy noise. Seamus remembered coming upon Katie's mother, dead and cold, her tiny cub crying out in distress. Katie had clung on to Seamus when he'd picked her up, her mouth seeking food from his shirt. She'd become Seamus's right then and there. He couldn't abandon her, and he knew it.

"Take Bree to safety," Seamus said to Broderick. "And let us go. Those are my terms."

"Screw that." Bree faced Broderick, hands on hips. "Go away and leave them the hell alone, all right? Why can't you pesky Shifters mind your own business?"

Broderick didn't look intimidated. "What, are you going to slap me on the nose, like you did Dylan?" The air vibrated with his chuckle. "I'd have paid to see that." His gaze returned to Seamus. "There's no choice, my friend. I know you're waiting to join up with Kendrick again, but he's not coming back. Not for a while. Dylan did something with him—we don't know what. We're trying to round up his Shifters, make sure they're all right. That means you three—unless there's more of you hiding in the basement?"

Seamus's mouth went dry, Broderick's last words fading into garbled syllables. Dylan had captured Kendrick? When? How? Kendrick was as hard-ass and dominant as Dylan was—he wouldn't simply lay down his sword and bow his head, not even to Dylan. Kendrick was a good leader. He'd never leave his Shifters to fend for themselves.

Francesca was furious. "You seriously want us to believe that?"

Broderick gave her a nod. "I've got one of the un-Collared ones from your bunker living in my house already." He grimaced. "Mate of my girlfriend's sister. Well, maybe she's my girlfriend. This Shifter, he's half feral, and we're nursing him back to health. He's driving me batshit crazy, and I can't wait until he's better and *out* of there. But what do you do? My girlfriend would kill me if I tossed him out while he's still nuts."

Seamus knew exactly which Shifter he was talking about. A Feline called Aleck had started to deteriorate into the feral state they all feared. He'd hooked up with a groupie one night—Nancy, Seamus thought her name was. She'd stayed with him, helping him. Aleck had disappeared the night Kendrick's compound had been raided.

Now Broderick was saying Aleck was at *his* house. In a Shiftertown.

"How is he?" Seamus couldn't stop the question.

"Aleck?" Broderick considered. "Better. Being with Nancy helps him. We're hoping we won't have to put a real Collar on him—Sean thinks it might make him worse. But we're working on it."

Seamus felt the weight of Francesca's gaze. She was waiting for him to make the decision, to choose whether they'd let these Shifters take them or fight it out.

Shite. There was Katie to consider. If Seamus let the Collared Shifters have her, she'd be stuck in a Shiftertown the rest of her life. She'd never be allowed to leave. Katie's mother had fled her Shiftertown to have Katie, presumably hoping Katie would be forever free. Could Seamus break the silent promise he'd given to the dead woman to make sure Katie was unharmed and happy?

On the other hand, where would Seamus take Katie now? If Broderick spoke the truth, and Kendrick wasn't coming for them, at least not right now, then Seamus needed to find another place for her. But he sure as hell didn't know where.

He'd put together the safe houses while he'd been living in the compound, against the day they'd have to flee. He'd been careful, finding places that were abandoned or secluded, making cash deals under the table with the owners when he needed to.

All his hiding places were burned now. Bree's house likewise was compromised. Seamus could take Francesca and Katie and run for it, but they'd have to get past Broderick and Tiger. Seamus was willing to bet there were more Shifters outside, like Spike and Ronan, waiting to sweep them up if they ran.

The indecision—or the futility of his choices— nudged the feral in him to life. Seamus felt the surge of adrenaline, his fight-or-flight instinct rising to take over. He could fight, kill, run. He turned slowly to Broderick, feeling his body ripple, wanting to change, his sight shifting to his lion's.

The world took on curved edges, slightly fuzzy. With that curving vision, Seamus saw Broderick straightening, coming alert, his wolf's eyes tinged with red. Fight, crush, break, *kill* ...

A touch jerked him away from the spinning thoughts. Seamus looked down to see Bree next to him. The only thing left of her cat makeup was smudges around her eyes, a bit of black on the tip of her nose.

Her scent was warm. Violets, he'd thought last night. Now she was more honey-like, tinged with lemon.

Bree's blue eyes held him, pulling him in. He could drown in that blue.

"Seamus," she was saying, her voice soft. "I've hung out with a lot of Shifters. I stalk them, remember?" Her little smile tore at him. "One thing I've learned is that no matter how wild they get, or how badass they pretend to be, Shifters don't hurt the cubs. They protect them against the entire world. Humans, Shifter Bureau, other Shifters. If there's a safe place for Katie to be, it's a Shiftertown."

Seamus's mouth was stiff, but he made himself answer. He was surprised he could still talk. "Once she goes in, she'll never be let out."

"Hey, we're working on that," Broderick said. He spoke calmly, but his wary stance hadn't changed, and he wasn't taking his eyes off Seamus. "Shifters won't be captives forever. At least, that's what the Morrisseys are always spouting. I know you all liked living in your crazy-ass underground bunker with no windows, but someday, we're going to walk around in the light without Collars. You want to be around when that happens?"

"Sounds like a speech you've made before," Seamus said.

"Yeah, well, you got me. I'm not good with words. And you should hear my girlfriend complain about *that*. Anyway, it sounds better than *Come with us or we tranq you and take you anyway*. Doesn't it? You don't have a choice, my friend."

"I think Tiger already decided," Bree broke in. "And I think Katie likes him."

Tiger had climbed silently to his feet and was making for the door. Katie clung to Tiger's back, her dark eyes sparkling with excitement.

Tiger didn't wait for anyone to get out of his way. He just went. Bree and Francesca had to scuttle aside, and Broderick stepped quickly into the hall as Tiger moved through the door. Broderick didn't try to stop Tiger or even talk to him.

Broderick *did* try to stop Seamus going after Tiger, stepping in front of him as Seamus left the room. Seamus abruptly shoved the Lupine against the nearest wall. He saw the flare of fighting rage in Broderick's gray eyes, and then Broderick's deliberate decision not to do battle, not right now.

Seamus released him and skimmed down the stairs, Bree behind him. Tiger was already in the kitchen, making his silent, swift way out of the house, Katie hanging on to his back.

Seamus charged out of the house ... and straight into a ring of waiting Shifters. Ronan, Sean the Guardian, Spike of the many tattoos, another Lupine dressed like a cowboy. Seamus sensed more Shifters in the front of the house, others hidden all around the property. They were taking no chances.

Tiger simply walked past them, carrying Katie away. Ronan, the bear Shifter, lifted a tranq rifle and pointed it at Seamus.

Bree barreled out of the house behind him. "Wait! Don't shoot him!"

Sean gave Ronan a nod and spoke in his dark, Irish-accented voice. "Stand down, Ronan. I don't think we'll be needing that."

"No," Seamus said. The word held finality, and also great sadness. "You won't."

Chapter Twelve

They rode to Shiftertown in a series of vehicles. The cowboy, Ellison, who introduced himself to Bree with the tip of his hat and a big smile, drove a black pickup with Tiger hunkered in the back, covered by a tarp. Katie was under there with him, with Francesca, who refused to go unless she could stay with Katie.

Sean had Seamus and Bree ride in a small white pickup with him. The others came on motorcycles or trucks, none of them pulling out of the neighborhood at the same time. They dispersed, rather than riding in a convoy.

"We'll have to figure out where to put you all," Sean said, sounding cheerful as he turned onto a street that headed downtown. It wasn't a main street, and Bree wasn't sure where they were.

"Katie will probably go in with Ronan and the bears," Sean went on. "Ronan and Rebecca foster orphaned cubs, and they know how to take care of little bears, who can be a handful, I don't mind telling you. We *might* have room for you, Seamus, at our place, but you'd have to live with Dylan, and even scarier, Glory. You haven't lived until you've stumbled into Glory first thing in the morning before she's had her coffee. My brother, Liam, might be able to squeeze you in, but Tiger lives in his house, and so does Tiger's mate, who's expecting. But don't worry, we'll find somewhere." Sean relayed all this while zipping expertly through the narrow streets, heading ever eastward. "You, Bree, already have a home. Unless you want to stay with Seamus ..."

He left it hanging. Bree knew Sean had sensed something between her and Seamus — all right, they'd made it pretty damn obvious. She had no idea how far it would go. Would Seamus flee once Katie was safe? What room would he have in his life for Bree?

"What happened at my house?" she asked Sean around Seamus. "When we left, the cops were ready to take you in. Apparently, they didn't. Is my mom all right?"

"That she is," Sean said. "Dylan went to the station with the police — his suggestion. He's good at talking people 'round, is Dad. But we'll discuss it when we get home." Sean shot Bree a look. "Your mum's almost as scary as Glory, you know? I drove her to Shiftertown."

Bree's eyes widened. "You took my mother to *Shiftertown*?" She gave a mock shudder, hiding her relief that for now, her mom was okay. "You're right; that is scary."

"She wouldn't stay home until we guaranteed that you were well. So Dylan made the call, and we took her with us to Shiftertown. She's fine, only a *little* put out that she can't smoke."

"Oh." Bree rubbed the bridge of her nose. "In that case, she might explode."

"She's waiting for you at Liam's house. Your mum was a bit more obliging about the smoking when she saw that Tiger's mate was pregnant, and that Liam has a wee one underfoot. She decided the smoke would be bad for Carly and the cubs — but *she* decided, mind. If your mum was a Shifter, I bet she'd give every alpha a run for their money."

Bree had to agree. She squeezed Seamus's thigh where he sat between her and Sean. He put his hand on hers, and Bree didn't pull away. They rode into Shiftertown, fingers entwined.

***

Seamus had never been to a Shiftertown. He'd avoided them with every breath, making sure he never came within miles of them. Now he was heading rapidly toward one.

This Shiftertown was to the east of the 35, near the old airport. While Mueller was now being built up with houses and offices, large stretches of it still remained empty or half demolished. The Shiftertown was north of that, in neighborhoods as hidden as the one they'd just left.

They passed a bar Sean said was a favorite hangout and turned into the streets of the neighborhood. Seamus's breath stuck in his chest. He couldn't move, couldn't think. A haze rose before his eyes, which obscured the trees, bungalows, and Shifters.

It was dusk, the sun setting early in the winter. Lights were on in windows and porches, Shifters coming outside—most Felines and Lupines were nocturnal.

All stopped to watch Sean's white truck, and Ellison's black one, which had caught up to them, coming slowly down the road. They knew. The whole town.

Shifter communities were like that. Seamus never understood how it worked, but news flashed from one Shifter to another with astonishing speed. A growl here, a look there, and rumor could flow faster than a Shifter could run.

The streets were quiet, no traffic at all, though vehicles were parked at curbs or in driveways. The houses were old bungalows with deep porches, neatly kept yards, no fences. Large trees overhung the houses, trimmed, but thick enough to hide whatever Feline Shifter in big cat form might have climbed into one to rest on a branch.

Sean pulled to a halt in front of a two-story bungalow with concrete strips that served as a driveway. Trees towered in the yard, obscuring the top of the house. Kids' toys littered the porch, Seamus saw as he climbed the steps, following Sean, his heart pounding, though an attempt had been made to order them in the corner. A Shifter cub lived here.

Bree was directly against Seamus's back, but she looked around with interest. Her presence was the only thing keeping Seamus calm. Every fear he'd ever had in his life was swamping him, telling him to run, to fight his way free. Only Bree's touch and his concern for Katie kept him in place.

Tiger was out of the black truck as soon as it stopped. Francesca climbed out after him, rubbing her arms and looking around in suspicion and fear.

Katie barreled out from under the tarp and landed on Tiger's back. Seamus started for them, worried about what Tiger would do when the small missile landed on him, but all Tiger did was glance once at Katie as though making sure she was secure. He then walked up the steps of the bungalow, ignoring Seamus.

The front door opened, letting out a warm square of light, and a tall Shifter looked out at them. Tiger, without waiting for invitation, walked right inside.

"Come on in," the Feline Shifter in the doorway said, his Irish accent mirroring Sean's. "I'm Liam. You're welcome in my house."

I'm opening my territory to you, he meant. *But you're here on my sufferance until I know you better. Be careful.*

Seamus acknowledged this with a nod. *Your territory. Your rules.*

Liam returned the acknowledgment without having to speak or even make a gesture. Seamus found it very easy to understand this man, as he had with Sean and Dylan. But then, they were all lions together. The tiger and the tattooed Spike were still enigmas.

Seamus stepped into the house, following Liam, drawing Bree with him. The house was full, and Seamus's shyness kicked in. He wasn't used to being around so many strangers.

He knew he'd never remember all their names right away, so for now he didn't bother to try. The important ones were Liam; his mate, Kim, who was human; a tall blond female Shifter — Glory — who was Dylan's mate; and Carly, human and very pregnant.

The two human women converged on Bree. "Hey," Carly said. She had honey-colored hair, a wide smile, and an abdomen that announced her cub was growing large. "Welcome to the neighborhood, honey. I bet these Shifters have been running you ragged, not even offering you a glass of something. Come on. Kim and I will fix you up."

Tiger slid between the three of them, his big head rubbing on Carly's extended belly. Carly rumpled his fur and played with his ear, something Seamus couldn't imagine a sane person doing. She was his mate, all right.

"Aw, look what Tiger's brought us," Carly said, her gaze on Katie. "A cutie, cutie cub."

Another little girl with black curly hair shot out from the kitchen. "Tigger!" she cried, her arms outstretched. She stopped short and stared at the bear cub. "Who's that?"

Bree answered her. "This is Katie. Isn't she the sweetest thing? Who are *you*?"

"K'triona," the small girl answered. "I'm going to be a lion. Like him." She pointed a finger at Seamus.

Francesca had halted at Seamus's side. She shivered, her terror and uncertainty palpable. Seamus put an arm around her, rubbing her shoulder and coaxing her to relax. Difficult to, when his own awareness was one of crackling tension.

The next hour was chaotic. Nadine was there, mother and daughter embracing then talking at the same time. Seamus couldn't hear what they said, their words drowned out by the voices of the male Shifters surrounding Seamus and Francesca.

Liam, who looked laid-back and uninterested in the world, proved to be anything but. The gleam in his blue eyes told Seamus he was every bit as formidable as Dylan. If Seamus wanted to escape Shiftertown, it would be *this* man he'd have to get past, didn't matter how big Tiger, Ronan, and the others were.

Bree and her mom were now drinking wine with Kim, Carly sticking to water. Bree had been absorbed into the group, already laughing and talking as though she and these women who'd mated with Shifters had been friends forever. Human females could do that. Shifter females, like Francesca, were going to need more time.

Seamus knew Francesca wanted to shift, to fight, to flee. She was holding herself back, only because she knew she'd never win, and she'd do nothing to jeopardize Katie. As it was, she would not stray a step from Seamus.

That changed when Ronan arrived with more women, two of whom were human—his mate and her sister. Mate and sister joined the ladies in wine and laughter. The sister, who had hair streaked hot pink and orange, was already hanging on to Bree.

"Oh, sweetie, your top is *darling*. I wish I'd known you liked Shifter bars; I could have gone with you. You'd have had a great time. Some of those girls can be real bitches, but once you get past them, it's fun."

Her sister, Elizabeth, gave her a severe look. "Mabel, what did we talk about you going to the roadhouses?"

Mabel rolled her eyes. "Please, I'm a grown woman." *Barely*, Seamus thought. "Besides, I go with Connor, and everything's fine."

The tall nephew of Liam and Sean, who looked to be a few years younger than Transition age, joined the group. "Now, don't go telling tales on me," Connor said. "Uncle Liam and Uncle Sean will be putting me in a cage."

The third female who'd come with Ronan was definitely Shifter. A bear, Seamus figured, a big one. She was of Ronan's clan, he sensed by the way they were together, but she was mated to the human male in black fatigues at her side.

This Shiftertown was crazy.

"Tell you what," the she-bear, Rebecca, said to Seamus and Francesca. "I'll take you over to our place. We'll introduce Katie to our family, and fix up rooms for you. Katie's going to get too upset with all this ruckus."

Francesca folded her arms, trying to hunker in on herself. "What's to say Katie won't get upset being with *you*?"

"Because we have bear cubs too," Rebecca said. "She'll fit right in. We have the best and biggest bear house in Shiftertown."

Rebecca's dominance was clear. But though the man with her might be human, he wasn't her second. He was quiet because he chose to be.

"Who are you?" Seamus asked him.

The man, Walker Danielson, with his pale, buzzed hair and light blue eyes, met Seamus's gaze with a strong one. "Shifter Bureau."

Seamus's feral instincts rose again, the haze, which had cleared a bit when meeting Shifters who seemed friendly if wary, returned. He turned to Sean. "You brought in *Shifter Bureau*? What the hell have you done to me?"

"Nothing," Walker said before Sean could answer. "But we need to talk."

***

Bree's new best friends and her mother tried to get her to stay at Liam and Kim's house while Seamus took Katie away with the bears. Bree said a firm—"Sorry, want to make sure everything's cool," and walked away from them.

The young women she'd just met were much like the girlfriends Bree had left behind in New Orleans. A warmth began behind her breastbone. It was nice to find like-minded ladies to talk to after being lonely for so long.

However, Bree didn't want to stay there and lose sight of Seamus and Katie. She knew these Shifters would be good to the cub, despite Francesca's and Seamus's fears, but she was worried about Seamus. She couldn't shake the feeling that if she let him walk away, she'd never see him again.

Carly had said that the man, Walker, was Shifter Bureau, though she said it without concern. "He'll leave you alone, sweetie," Carly reassured her. "Just mention duct tape."

The others went off into laughter, telling Bree there was a story there, but she didn't have time to hear it now.

Tiger accompanied Seamus and Bree to the bear's home, Katie riding on his back again. Rebecca led the way with her long stride, her voice and Walker's entwining. They bantered, they laughed — well, Rebecca laughed loudly while Walker's laughter was quieter and more subdued.

A true couple, Bree thought wistfully. Without doubt.

The house they approached was large, square, two-story, set well back from the street, and surrounded by trees. More Shifters came outside as they approached, but these were younger, eager and hanging back at the same time. Cubs, three of them.

One was a young man who was well built and more confident than the others. A full adult in Shifter terms, but not by much, Bree guessed, maybe just past what they called the Transition. The young woman was about Mabel's age, early twenties, but in Shifter terms, she was still a true cub. The boy with white hair looked to be about ten or eleven.

Francesca hung back, but Katie had no uncertainty. She slid off of Tiger, landed heavily, rolled to her feet, and bounded up to the porch.

The little boy leaned down to her. Bree sensed the others tense, as though waiting to see what he'd do.

The boy studied the bear cub, porch lights shining on white hair and black eyes that were like pieces of the night. Katie sat down on her hindquarters and stared right back at him.

"What's her name?" the boy asked without looking away from her.

Francesca cleared her throat. "She's Katie. She's an orphan."

"Like me," the boy said. "Hello, Katie. I'm Olaf."

Katie blinked some more, then she got to her feet and bumped her head into the boy's thin legs. Olaf put his arms around Katie and hugged her.

Katie made one of her contented, growly noises and hugged him back. Bree sensed the other Shifters relax, as though something important had just happened.

Olaf straightened and looked around at the waiting adults. "She's very little," he said. "Can I take care of her?"

"Of course you can, sweetie," Rebecca said, her voice warming as she moved to the porch. "Let's take her inside, all right?"

***

"Time for some serious talk," Walker said.

Bree seated herself at the long table in Ronan's house, folded her hands, and proceeded to listen. She *did* trust these Shifters—at least, more than Seamus did—but if they even mentioned putting a Collar on Seamus or caging him, they were going to hear it from her. She wasn't quite sure what she could do against them, if anything, but she wouldn't let them hurt Seamus—or Katie or Francesca—without a fight.

Walker Danielson reminded Bree strongly of her brother, though Walker was quieter. Remy, while a hard partier, had possessed the same competent strength, the same air of self-assurance that led others to follow him. Sadness touched her, but at the same time, thinking about her brother gave her confidence.

Walker had tried to suggest that Bree go back to the Morrisseys, or at least retired to the room upstairs she'd been given, to get some rest. Bree refused. They were going to talk about what to do about Seamus, and she wasn't going anywhere.

Seamus didn't sit down but wandered the room, restless. Rebecca had taken Francesca and the cubs to what she called the Den, the converted garage where she and Walker lived. Walker had remained behind, and Ronan had returned without his mate but with Dylan.

Dylan had spent the afternoon with the police, Walker told them, convincing them that his Shifters had nothing to do with the deaths of the hunters. Walker had met him there to help, the police more trusting of a human who worked for Shifter Bureau.

Now the three, Walker, Dylan, and Ronan, faced Seamus.

"The only way to clear this up," Walker said, "is to find out who did kill those hunters. If it was a Shifter, he needs to be stopped."

Seamus ceased his pacing. Bree saw his distress in his tight back and shoulders, the haunted look in his golden eyes. "It might have been me," he said. Pain filled his voice. "I just don't know. I think I'm going feral."

"Fighting frenzy happens," Dylan said, his blue eyes intent upon Seamus. "Whether you wear a Collar or not. Collars just make it hurt more."

"No," Seamus said tightly. "I mean I think I'm going feral, *right now*."

Chapter Thirteen

Seamus could barely see, barely think. The presence of Ronan, Walker, and Dylan—a bear, a human, and an alpha Feline—was making him insane.

Bree sat alone at the table, a bright smudge of light in the middle of darkness. The three males, enemies to keep from his mate.

Seamus went to Bree's chair and slid it back with her in it, putting himself between her and the others. Dylan and Walker watched him, their stances betraying their tension.

Only the bear, Ronan, remained comfortable and unworried. "You sure it's *fighting* frenzy that's wrong with him?" he asked in his deep voice.

"Feral." Seamus heard the snarl in his voice. "I can't keep it contained. Lock me up somewhere. Don't let me hurt Bree."

Bree was up and out of the chair, her cool hands on Seamus's hot skin. "Seamus, I'm not going to let them do anything to you."

Seamus suppressed a shudder, Bree's touch the only thing anchoring him to the present. "Bree, love." He turned her to him, brushed shaking fingers over her cheek. "I might have killed those men. I was attacked, I responded. The next thing I knew they were torn apart. I don't want to wake up and find out I've done that to you."

Bree was supposed to look at him in terror, run from him, go far away where he'd never find her. That's what human women did when Shifters frightened them. No matter how much groupies pretended to be fascinated by Shifters, at some point the excitement was over, and true danger began.

Bree closed her hands around Seamus's forearms and drew herself closer to him. "I *know* you didn't kill them. You don't have it in you."

Seamus knew he should jerk away, put the distance of the room between them, demand Walker to hurry up and take her out of there. Instead, he stepped to her, letting their bodies touch.

"How do you know?" he asked in a fierce voice. "You only met me last night. I was bloody and shot up, and I forced you to help me get away. How can you say I don't have it in me?"

Bree's look was far too calm. "Because I know. Listen, everyone thought my brother was a total fuck-up. That he was dangerous, nothing but trouble. They said it so much that Remy started to believe it himself. That's why he joined the army, to prove he was a good guy at heart. But *I* knew it already. Remy always went out of his way to make sure I was all right, that my mom was. My dad died when I was five—I barely remember him. But Remy was always there, taking care of us. Shit happened *around* him, and people blamed it on him, but it wasn't him starting fires or wrecking cars—he was the best driver I ever met. He started driving at thirteen, because how else were we going to get groceries when my mom had to work twelve-hour shifts? He took care of us."

She paused, but she didn't let go. "I look at you, and see the same thing in you," Bree went on. "Everything you've done, you've done to take care of Francesca and Katie. You're still doing it. And now you're taking care of me as well."

He didn't so much hear Bree's individual words as the sound of her voice. It flowed over him, her scent and touch calming him.

"It's different for Shifters," Seamus said, words coming with difficulty. "We're not human. We're animal first. That animal always wants to take over. It's how we were bred. We want to fight, to kill. It's our nature. We fight it so we can survive, have cubs, and continue."

Bree shook her head. "It doesn't matter." She ran her hands up him arms. "You're a fighter, sure, and you're good at sneaking around, but you're not a killer. I do know about Shifters—my friend in Louisiana had a blog I contributed to, we researched, we had chats with people all over the world about Shifters, people who knew a lot of stuff. Heck, everything that happened last night and today would have made a great post, but I won't write it because it would put you in danger, something I'd never do. My point is that I've learned about all kinds of Shifters for years. The feral ones aren't like you. *You* are exhausted, worried, living on adrenaline, while you try to make sure everyone's all right. These are bad circumstances. I know that—"

"*Bree.*" Seamus put his fingertips to her lips. "What you and your groupie friends know about Shifters is the tip of the iceberg."

"I don't know," Ronan said. "I've read some of those blogs. They're pretty good. Helping make Shifters look fun. 'Cause, you know, we are."

Seamus ignored him. "I blanked out—my instinct to protect Katie kicked in and wiped out everything. I don't know what happened exactly. But if I did kill those men, I can't know if it won't happen again. I might hurt other Shifters. Cubs. *You.*"

Bree's hold tightened. "No, you won't. When you jumped into my truck and told me to get you away, you could have hurt me. You could have pushed me out, stolen the truck, left me to fend for myself. You could have forced me to drive off into a field, killed me, taken off. You didn't do any of those things. You came to my house, put up with my mother, for heaven's sake, protected us. When my mom picked those bullets out of you, you *sat* there. I'd think that pain would have made you go feral if you were heading that way. And Fuzzles liked you."

Seamus tried to clear his head. "Fuzzles?"

"Our cat. She doesn't like just anyone. She was all over you the second she laid eyes on you." Bree ran her hands up his arms again, which were whole, if scarred. "Can't say I blame her."

The rest of the world, the Shifters, Walker, the threats, Seamus's fears, abruptly spun away. Seamus saw only Bree, her blue eyes, her round face and wisps of golden hair, her plump lips that curved with her smile.

Seamus slid his hands to her waist, the tight skirt beckoning his touch. He moved his palms down her spine to cup her backside, soft through the leather.

Bree's breath quickened, warm on his lips. Seamus, still in the world where nothing existed but her, leaned down and kissed her.

A slow kiss, taking his time. It was a kiss of need, and also of possession, telling the other Shifters in the room that Bree was *his*.

Bree kissed him back, her arms coming around him as she opened to him thoroughly, making a low noise in her throat. She scooped herself to him, breasts and hips fitting to his chest and thighs.

The kiss turned fierce, Bree pulling him closer. Heat skimmed down Seamus's body and rested in his cock.

He wanted to explore her, get to know her, find out everything about her. Every curve, every corner, every part of her. He wanted to lay Bree down and feel her beneath him, slide inside her, let her make him whole again.

"You could be right, Ronan," came Walker's slow drawl. "Maybe not *fighting* frenzy."

They weren't wrong. Seamus wanted them all to vanish into the blue and leave him alone with Bree. So they could be together, on the table, on the carpet, on that big couch over there ...

"I'm taking you back to the scene," Dylan announced, his voice like a glacier. "The sooner we figure out what happened, the sooner I can make the police happy. After that, you can deal with your mating need."

"Even Dylan has to respond to mating need," Ronan put in. "Glory makes sure he does."

For the first time, Seamus heard Dylan's tone soften. "Shut it, Ronan."

Bree pressed her hands flat against Seamus's chest and pushed. Seamus reluctantly broke the kiss. He didn't let her go, though, pulling her closer. Shifters needed touch, and Seamus needed it right this second.

"Yes, let's go figure out what happened," Bree said. She rose on tiptoes and whispered into Seamus's ear. "And then *you* can teach me all about mating frenzy."

***

Seamus did not want to be in the cab of the white pickup one more time, heading south in the dark, out of Austin and to the area around the roadhouse. Walker drove, while Ronan and Dylan rode in the bed, lounging easily.

While Dylan had assured Seamus that the humans had finished with the scene of the killings for now and wouldn't be anywhere near, that wasn't the point. Seamus worried that simply being in the vicinity of the fight would trigger his feral state, make him the crazed fighting beast he'd become.

He had the feeling that this was exactly what Dylan wanted. What better way to prove Seamus was going feral than to try to trigger it?

Bree was next to Seamus, holding his hand. They'd been doing so almost since they'd met, Seamus mused. As though they'd instinctively known they had to hold on to each other, no matter what.

Not letting go, Seamus vowed. *Never letting go.*

They passed the roadhouse, which was already going for the night, lights flooding the parking lot. Shifters and humans milled in and out of the lit open doorway.

Walker drove on, taking a turnoff at Seamus's direction to head toward Seamus's safe house. Seamus had been attacked somewhere between the safe house and the bar, though he wasn't quite certain where. Darkness and disorientation had added to his confusion.

Walker turned off on a dirt road, going down a slight rise that would hide them from the main highway. At the very end of this road was another, narrower road that led to the house, abandoned long ago. The farm that had lain around it was now fields of dust.

Dylan told Walker to stop the pickup some way before they made the house. Walker pulled to a halt, shutting off the engine and lights.

The silence out here was breathtaking. No cars, people, dogs, not even air traffic passing overhead interrupted the peace. The sky above was thick with stars, as though nothing blocked the way to those distant suns. Here you could see stars *between* the stars.

Seamus had selected the house for its isolation. He'd hear anyone coming a long way off, soon enough for them to go to ground if necessary.

And yet there had been something wrong. They'd spent several weeks there, Seamus and Francesca taking turns uneasily walking the perimeter while Katie slept or played.

Finally, one morning Seamus had decided to move them. Francesca hadn't argued. He'd sensed that hiding out in the middle of the city would be more effective than sitting here alone, waiting for an attack.

"I had a pickup stashed about a mile away," Seamus said, breaking the stillness, though no one had asked him a question. "I drove Francesca and Katie to the house in Austin, then I came back alone. I wanted to make sure I hadn't led whoever it was straight to them. I ditched the truck on the outskirts of Austin and returned to the house across country. I prowled around, acting like we were still staying there."

A light flared, Dylan flicking on a powerful flashlight. Though Shifters could see in the dark, the two humans could not very well, plus Dylan was looking for minute evidence.

"The bodies were here," Dylan said, shining the light over the area. "The police brought me out here earlier, hoping I could solve the riddle for them. Shotguns torn apart, as were the men."

Dylan spoke clinically, but Seamus couldn't forget the stench of death, the horror of blood and entrails, the kick of feeling that he wasn't alone.

"This smells wrong," Seamus said abruptly. "This isn't where I found them."

The others lifted their heads from studying the ground. Bree hadn't left Seamus's side, and she looked up at him now. "What do you mean?" she asked.

Seamus's heart beat faster. "Nothing in this exact spot triggers my memories. Even if I never remember, I'd at least catch my own scent. The bodies were moved here *after* I ran from the hunters."

Dylan gave a nod. "That's what I thought too — that they'd been killed elsewhere. I looked for a trail, evidence that they were dragged or carried in a vehicle, but found nothing. It was plenty bloody here, so whoever brought them tore them up a little more when they dumped them here."

"But it wasn't me." Seamus's body relaxed so fast he feared his knees would buckle. "I was never here."

Walker broke in, his matter-of-fact tone reminding Seamus that the solution was not that simple. Seamus still could have done the original murder, with another Shifter dragging the bodies from the scene. "Tell us what you do remember."

Seamus ran a shaky hand over his hair. "Other hunters were coming — they'd seen me standing over the bodies. I ran to the roadhouse parking lot. We should backtrack from the roadhouse, see if we can find the place the men were actually killed."

"Let's do it then," Dylan said. He snapped off the light and made for the truck.

Walker drove them past the roadhouse again and turned off onto a dirt road that circled it. He certainly knew his way around back here, but maybe Shifter Bureau made him patrol the area.

Walker stopped the truck. They were far enough from the roadhouse that the parking lot's lights wouldn't reach them but close enough so Seamus could search out his route.

Seamus's heart was squeezing as he climbed out of the truck, beating so hard it felt like it was trying to jump up his gullet. Sensations rushed back at him—scents, the sounds of screaming, shouting, blood, darkness, pain. Rage so vast it could not be his.

"There was something in the dark with me," he said, his throat raw. He still had hold of Bree's hand—he should release her and not make her go through this, but he couldn't seem to let go. He walked with her unerringly down a dry ditch, which was thick with dust at the bottom. "Here," he said.

The blood smell was acrid, cloying. Ronan let out a whistle. "Goddess, that's ripe."

Walker and Bree, though they didn't have Shifter sensitivity to smell, both backed up a pace, Bree wrinkling her nose.

"I agree, this is where it must have happened." Dylan seemed the only one not affected by the smell. "The scents are right. The hunters were killed in this ditch then carried away, not dragged. Someone very strong did that. The killer didn't bother to come back and clean up the scene. Buzzards have been here, just because of the blood."

They'd have left disappointed, Seamus thought. No bones to pick.

The dizziness that had been bothering him returned with a whack. Seamus clamped down on Bree's hand, his breathing shallow.

"No, don't let me ..."

"You're not going anywhere," Bree said quickly. She squeezed his hand. "I'm right here. I'm not letting you go feral, or be taken to Shifter prison, or anything else. I know you didn't kill the hunters."

"There was anger," Seamus said. "Despair. So much of it. Killing rage. It came at me, swept me up in it. I fought." The impact of the attack came back to him, the noise and fury. "I fought hard, shifted—it was in between-beast form. It threw me aside, beat me down again and again. I couldn't protect them ..."

Bree's touch was the only thing that kept him connected to the present. Without it, Seamus would have swirled inside his memories and not come out. His awareness of her, like a beacon at his side, grounded him, allowing him to speak of it and not relive it.

"I tried to protect them, and then they were dead."

"Protect who?" Bree asked in her soft voice. "The hunters?"

"Yes." Seamus gazed down at her, her eyes in the starlight the only thing worth looking at. "Stupid humans. Stalking a Shifter, trying to kill it. Not me. They were stalking the other Shifter, who was after *me*. He was feral. Whatever is feral in me tried to become like him. It was so real, so vivid, I couldn't tell where he left off and I began. It was too tempting to give in to the wildness. For a moment, I was completely gone. Feral. Never coming back. Dear Goddess, it was one of the worst moments of my life. To know I was insane, dangerous, a killer ... and not to care."

Chapter Fourteen

"But you weren't." Bree's hand tightened on his. "You didn't kill those men. You made it to find me. I helped you, and you helped me. You came back from it."

Seamus dragged in a long breath, finding the cool sweetness of the night beyond the blood. "Yes. I came back. But the other hunters thought the killer was me. *I* thought I was."

And so they'd chased him, shooting, ready to bring him down.

"Well, that's a relief," Ronan broke in, cutting through Seamus's horror. "Won't have to kill you then. I kind of like you, Feline."

Seamus reached for grim humor. "Good thing. I'm sleeping in your house tonight."

"Bree," Dylan said abruptly. "How long were you were in the roadhouse?"

"Um." Bree pursed her lips as she thought. Red, sweet-tasting lips. Now that Seamus knew—or mostly knew—what had happened, his thoughts were turning to his other pull. The need for Bree.

"I'd say a little over an hour." Bree said. "I ordered one drink and looked for someone to talk to. Shifters were standoffish there."

Ronan nodded. "They don't much like strangers. Come to Liam's bar. We're much more friendly. I'm the bouncer—I make *sure* everyone's more friendly."

Seamus pictured Bree in the small bar they'd passed on the way to Shiftertown, swaying to music in her tight skirt, while Shifters vied to get next to her. He growled and tightened his hold on her.

Bree didn't seem to mind. She answered Dylan, "If you're asking me if I saw any Shifters in the bar who might have killed the hunters, I don't think so. None of the Shifters there looked insane—well, not obviously, anyway. They were all Collared and comfortable with each other, as much as Shifters of different species from different Shiftertowns can be. If one was feral, I'm sure they would have noticed."

Dylan only grunted and gave her a nod of thanks.

"Which leaves us where?" Walker asked. He'd been quiet, waiting and listening. Seamus liked to do that too. "Are you saying there's an unknown, feral Shifter on the loose?"

"I want to go back to the safe house," Seamus said. "The one out here. When I was there, I *knew* something was wrong. I bet I was sensing the feral watching us. Watching *me*."

No one suggested that it was futile running around in the darkness. They went back to the truck, got in, and Walker drove away, following Seamus's directions again.

Ideas, thoughts, worries, swam in Seamus's brain. He tried to keep himself calm, tried to sort through them. The feral beast who'd attacked him had touched something feral inside him. Bree had told Seamus he wasn't a killer, and Seamus was starting to believe it. But something feral inside him had awakened, a disturbing wildness he couldn't ignore. *Something* was going on with him, and he needed to figure out what.

Bree's scent wrapped around him as Walker's truck bumped its way down the washboard road. She was *right* in a world that was wrong. A light in the darkness. Bree understood about grief, but she was living her life. The hole in that life, left by her brother's death, wasn't stopping her.

Seamus's need for her cried out to him, a craving so strong he could seize her now, leap out of the truck, and run off with her to some place where they could be together. Alone. Not surrounded by Shifters, hunters, killers, and a guy from Shifter Bureau.

Bree leaned against him, her sleek hair brushing his chin. Seamus slid his arms around her and rested his cheek on her head.

The safe house was difficult to see in the darkness, which was why Seamus had chosen it. It was a small house, abandoned, that must have stood here for fifty or sixty years. Seamus had shored it up and put in new windows and plumbing when he'd still lived in Kendrick's compound, fortifying it against a day he'd need it.

Other trackers had done similar things with the houses they used, but even the trackers didn't know where each other's safe houses were. Kendrick liked compartmentalization. If one tracker was compromised, he couldn't compromise them all.

Walker stopped where Seamus directed. Dylan took Seamus's key from him and led the way into the house, leaving Ronan to circle the place, looking for signs of intrusion. They'd found none so far. The place looked empty.

Even so, Dylan wanted to go first, his duty as strongest Shifter in the party to lead the way. Walker insisted on bringing up the rear, drawing a dark, thick-barreled pistol. Humans liked to do that, protecting from behind, which did make sense, especially with Bree between them.

The house, which consisted of two rooms and an attic, was empty. Seamus caught a whiff of his own scent—damn, he must have been nervous—Francesca, equally as nervous, and the rather soothing scent of baby Katie.

The aura of Katie's presence calmed Seamus. She was such a happy cub, in spite of her beginnings. But then, she'd been snatched away from death, cared for, loved. Katie enjoyed the hell out of her life. She was with Francesca now, in Shiftertown, as safe as she could be under the circumstances.

Over the scents of himself, Francesca, and Katie, Seamus detected the scent of another Shifter. The feral. Not strong—the feral wasn't there now—but Seamus's skin crawled. He felt his eyes change to his wildcat's, tension scraping his nerves raw.

They checked out the entirety of the small house, but found nothing. The Shifter hadn't left evidence of himself behind, nothing helpful like a note with directions to where he'd gone. The feral had come here, looked around, and departed.

They found no signs that Seamus and his charges had been living here either. Seamus hadn't left anything to betray their presence. He'd learned long ago the importance of being thorough.

Ronan came in the front door. "Hey, come see what I found," he said. Without another word, he turned around and faded back outside.

Seamus led the way this time, too impatient to wait for Dylan to play alpha. Ronan took them around the house to the back then moved some boards away from the foundation to show them a dark, gaping hole.

The scent that poured out of it was strong, fetid, disgusting. Seamus clapped his hand over his nose and mouth, and Ronan turned away, his face gray. Even Dylan backed a step or two, growls coming from his throat.

No one was there. Walker volunteered to go inside and look around, since his sense of smell wasn't as strong as the Shifters', and no one argued with him. The scent was making Seamus want to shift and get the hell out of there, and he knew Ronan had to be feeling the same way.

Walker flashed a light around inside then came back and hoisted himself out of the opening. "He used this space to access the inside of the house by popping out the floorboards above him," Walker announced as he climbed to his feet and dusted himself off. "Then replaced them when he left again. That's why the door was still locked, windows unbroken."

"What was he looking for?" Ronan asked. His voice sounded nasally as he tried to breathe only through his mouth. "Seamus? Or just a place to stay?"

"I don't know," Seamus said. "Unless he was one of Kendrick's Shifters, and went feral when we had to go to ground. That's what I thought was happening to me. He might have been looking for me to help him, but been too crazy to let me."

Dylan gave Seamus a thoughtful look. "I'm thinking there's more to this than we understand," he said. "But now that we know there's a rogue feral out there, I'll round up my trackers, and we'll hunt him. We'll find him."

"Let me join you," Seamus said. "If it *is* one of Kendrick's Shifters gone bad—I'll know him. He might respond to me." Seamus would try to help him—going feral was no Shifter's fault—but the guy had to be stopped. The feral was out of control, had murdered those men, and had tried to kill Seamus, not to mention leaving him to be blamed for the killings. Seamus didn't have a lot of sympathy for humans who hunted Shifters for sport, but they hadn't deserved such a death.

"Of course you're coming with us," Dylan said. "You'll know him when you encounter him, and I want to keep an eye on you."

Dylan and his trackers would hunt the Shifter, figure out who he was and what he was, and try to bring him back to sanity if they could.

If they couldn't, then they'd do what Shifters had to with ferals—end his life and send him to the Summerland. After that, Seamus would be free to discover what he had with Bree, to be with her.

Maybe. His fear that he might hurt Bree hadn't entirely gone. The feral should not have been able to drag Seamus into the madness with him.

Seamus also needed to figure out what had happened to Kendrick, what to do with Francesca and Katie, and whether Bree wanted a Collarless rogue Shifter to fall in love with her.

If he stayed in Shiftertown, what would happen to him? If he managed to escape, what about Bree? And Francesca and Katie?

Too many things. Seamus was a fighter, a soldier. He followed orders and left big decisions up to Shifters like Kendrick or Dylan.

Seamus had the feeling, though, that this time, the decisions had to come from him. And Bree. This was his *life*, not simply carrying out the orders of a leader. His brain hurt.

"You all right?" Bree asked, taking his hand as they walked back to the truck.

"No," he said. He drew her close, his arm stealing around her waist. "But it's better when I'm with you."

***

Back in Shiftertown, Bree filled Francesca in on what had happened, while Dylan had a quick conference in Ronan's living room with all the Shifters.

Bree heard Dylan and Walker relating what they'd found out at Seamus's safe house, then Dylan called the hunt to start in the morning, after they'd rested. Most feral Shifters reverted to being entirely nocturnal, Dylan said, and they would likely catch the Shifter napping—literally. Trackers from San Antonio had been recruited as well, Dylan finished, to watch the safe house tonight to see whether the feral returned. Dylan would be on alert, as would Liam and Sean.

After that, the trackers scattered, and Seamus nearly crashed to the floor.

Bree couldn't convince him to go to bed, though, until he was one-hundred percent certain that Katie would be all right. She'd been given a bed in the room with Cherie, a grizzly who was about twenty-one in human years, but still a cub in Shifter terms. Francesca would share the room as well, and Olaf insisted they set up a cot in it for him. He was determined to look after Katie. Seamus checked the room, the house, the Den, the yard, and the perimeter of the yard before he confessed himself satisfied, for now.

Finally, Bree dragged Seamus to bed.

No one questioned that Seamus and Bree would share a bedroom. The other Shifters only said good-night and trundled to their rooms to sleep, and Walker and Rebecca retired to the Den.

Bree had a low-voiced conversation with her mother after she marched Seamus upstairs—she had to use Ronan's land line in the kitchen, since Sean still hadn't returned her cell phone.

"Really, Mom, I'm fine. You sound like you're having a good time with Kim and Carly. We'll go home tomorrow. Tonight, I need to make sure Seamus is okay."

"Sure you do." Nadine skepticism floated over the phone. *"You know, I never thought my grandchildren would be Shifter, but if this is the only way I get any ..."*

Bree made a noise of exasperation. "Mom, you are so ahead of yourself. Good night."

"I'm just saying. Be careful over there."

"I'll talk to you tomorrow," Bree said firmly. "Good night."

"Good night, honey. Love you."

"Love you too." Bree said it in all sincerity. She and her mom had their ups and downs, but they'd survived a lot together, had made it because underneath their banter, they had a love that couldn't be broken.

Bree hung up the phone and walked upstairs and into the bedroom they'd been given, a small one that had belonged to Rebecca.

Seamus lay face down on the bed, sound asleep.

Bree closed the door and stood at the end of the bed, looking at him. Seamus was stretched out in exhaustion, one hand flung across the covers, the other hanging over the side of the mattress. He'd managed to get his boots and socks off, and his strong bare feet dangled off the bottom of the bed.

Bree had been able to wash up and brush her teeth with a toothbrush Ronan's mate had purchased for her, and now she stripped out of her clothes, sliding under the sheet in her bra and panties. She snapped off the light on the bedside table and snuggled down.

Seamus didn't move. A faint snore trickled into the room. Moonlight touched Seamus's tanned skin and danced in the darkness of his hair.

Bree had never seen him so relaxed. Since she'd met him, Seamus had been tense, wound to one focused point. He'd been afraid and trying to bottle up his fear to protect not only Katie and Francesca, but Bree as well. And her mom. Even the cat.

Bree leaned across the bed and kissed his cheek. She savored the warmth of his skin, the rough burn of his whiskers.

Seamus's eyes popped open. They glittered gold in the dark, a Shifter coming fully awake and alert.

Before Bree could say word, Seamus rose over her and bore her back into the bed. Bree found her arms full of strong-bodied Shifter, who covered her mouth with a slow but forceful kiss.

Seamus's mouth was a hot place, his lips both leisurely and intense, as though he planned to kiss her all night. Bree surrendered down into the mattress, ready to let him.

She tugged at his T-shirt, dragging it up so she could touch him. Seamus impatiently broke the kiss and shrugged the shirt off, then nearly ripped her bra's hooks to open it and fling it aside. Her underwear quickly followed.

Bare chest to bare chest, they came together, Seamus's heart beating hard above hers. Bree drew her fingers down Seamus's smooth back and slid them under the waistband, finding the taut mound of his buttocks beneath. No underwear. She'd thought as much.

"Need you," Seamus said. "Need you, my mate. Can't stop myself."

Bree didn't want him to. She worked her fingers around to the front of his jeans and popped open the button. The zipper hissed, and Bree plunged her hand inside to close it around his very hard cock.

Seamus froze. His eyes became a light golden color, as though he wanted to shift, and barely contained it. Or maybe he simply liked what she was doing. Bree stroked him once, enjoying how large he was. It would be a tight squeeze when he came inside her, but she wouldn't let that stop them.

She shoved at his jeans, which he got himself out of. Seamus kissed his way down her throat to her breasts, his warm mouth trickling heat across her flesh. Bree arched, wanting him.

"The whole of you," he said. He licked between her breasts. "You called out to me from the first. I belong ... with you."

"I'm not minding that," Bree whispered.

Seamus lifted away, repositioning himself to fit his body to hers. His cock brushed her opening, the already sensitive place shooting fires along every nerve.

So. This was being with a Shifter.

No, this was being with a man who was extraordinary, beautiful without knowing it, gentle and caring and at the same time, with an edge of unpredictability. His eyes took her in, the downward sweep of his gaze telling her he liked what he saw.

Bree smiled at him, liking him too. Seamus dragged in a breath, raised his hips, and slid inside her.

Large? *Yes.* Bree gasped as he filled her, opening pieces of her she hadn't realized were closed.

Seamus emitted a soft moan, his eyes flicking to Shifter, the gold of them vivid. Then he closed his eyes, his face relaxing even more as he began a sweet rhythm.

Bree wrapped her arms around him, twining her legs with his as he thrust into her, his first movements slow and sensual. The room was cool, November wind tapping at the window, but warmth swathed them. Bree pushed the sheet away.

Bare to the night, they loved each other, Seamus increasing his thrusts, Bree rising to meet him. He needed this; *she* needed it. Emptiness was flowing away, her heart healing for the first time in a long, long time.

Slow sensations fled as desperation came upon them, Seamus moving faster, Bree sliding hands to his buttocks, urging him on. Seamus's biceps bunched as he held himself from crushing her; Bree clung hard to him.

Madness was coming over her, a dark wash of climax—blissful, hot waves she gladly drowned in. She heard her voice rising, but everything went away, every worry, fear, and caution. All she knew was Seamus joining with her, spiraling her into a place of bright delight, one hot point of pleasure.

It lasted so long, both of them meeting in that place of fire, his shouts blending with hers. Just when Bree thought she'd never endure more—but *damn*, she did not want it to end—they crashed together on the bed, gasping, kissing, sealed together.

After a while, they eased into quietude, catching their breaths. Seamus smiled at her—the first time he'd done so. It was a wicked smile, one of both triumph and joy.

"Beautiful," he whispered as he came down to her. "I've never seen anything as beautiful as you."

"You're not bad yourself," Bree mumbled, exhaustion stealing her powers of speech. "In fact, you're pretty hot."

Seamus's low laughter shook the bed, and to this agreeable lullaby, Bree dropped into sleep.

***

A wild scream broke the darkness. Bree jumped awake, her heart banging.

The sound was more like a wail, a horrible noise that wound high, boring through Bree's brain. The sound came from outside, but an instant later, it was echoed by Seamus, who threw back his head and roared as though all the pain in the world had gathered within him.

Bree rolled away and scrambled to her feet in sheer panic. Seamus came off the bed, his hands on either side of his head, his eyes so light gold they were nearly white.

"Hurts," he moaned. "Hurts."

From outside came shouts, more screams, animal cries. Bree didn't want to take her gaze off Seamus, but she ran to the window and looked out.

Something crashed past the trees that lined the yard, a bulk running straight for the house. The Den was lit up, Walker outside. She heard the sound of a pistol shot, and another.

Seamus screamed again. Down below, Bree saw the glint of sword as Sean sprinted into the yard, with what looked like every male in Shiftertown behind him. They were chasing the giant animal that broke through Ronan's front door, splintering it, and charged into the house.

Chapter Fifteen

Pain. Emptiness. Rage.

All poured through Seamus as the feral came up the stairs, heading unerringly to what it needed.

The cub.

Screams sounded in the room where they'd put Katie—Cherie and Francesca, Olaf crying out. Seamus was barely aware of Bree snatching up his T-shirt to throw on her own body as he slammed himself out of the room and across the hall.

The door to Katie's room had been torn off its hinges. Seamus saw Cherie pressed into a far corner, her terror so high it cut through the rest of the emotions churning through Seamus's head.

That clarity allowed him to see the situation without the haze of madness—Francesca, her nightshirt fluttering to the floor as she shifted to wolf. Olaf, as small as he was, putting himself in front of Katie's bed, his hands out protectively.

Olaf faced another bear, its brown fur matted with mud and blood, giant paws sporting broken claws, its dark eyes filled with madness. The bear was male, Shifter, and feral. No Collar adorned its neck, Seamus saw in the moment the bear turned and came for him.

Seamus was already shifting to lion. The bear's attack caught him mid-shift, at his most vulnerable, which he now realized was how the bear had taken him by surprise out in the dark. Seamus spun back into the hall, his lion's hind legs scrabbling for purchase. Bree, wide-eyed, got out of the way.

Seamus gained his feet, fully lion now, and went for the bear. The bear hurtled out of the bedroom, and they slammed together in the hall.

The stink nearly knocked Seamus over, as did the feral's outpouring of grief, anger, and hatred. The bear struck, and struck again, its ragged claws raking Seamus's side. The scent of blood woke Seamus's frenzy, and then nothing was clear.

Teeth, claws, blows. Seamus rolled, with the bear on him, then he came up on top of the bear to be thrown aside like nothing. Francesca leapt, her wolf landing full force on the bear's back. At the same time Bree darted inside the room, heading to help the cubs.

Seamus was aware of other Shifters on their way up the stairs, Rebecca included, Walker behind her. Ronan had already charged out of his own room, but there was no space for him to shift into the Kodiak bear he was.

Another lion joined the fray. Seamus heard a sword clatter to the floor, and knew this was Sean. Sean hit the bear, driving it from Seamus, who rolled out from under it. Francesca ran at the bear's huge back feet, her wolf snapping and clawing.

Seamus saw the rage in the bear's eyes change to desperation. It knew it was outnumbered, would never get away. It flung off Seamus and Sean with renewed strength and burst into the bedroom.

Katie was standing on the bed, roaring in fear and surprise. On the floor next to her was a polar bear cub. He was up on his hind legs, his black eyes sparkling, his too-small mouth open in a warning roar. Cherie had turned grizzly, she too rising on back feet. Her bear was a little more formidable than those of the cubs, but she was still too young to take on the full-grown feral.

The feral bear drew back his huge paws and swept them down at Olaf and Katie. Seamus knew he'd never be able to reach them in time.

But Bree was there, rising from the other side of the bed like an avenging angel. She grabbed Katie and yanked her to safety, just as the bear's blow landed. The mattress ripped in two, and the wooden bedstead clattered apart, striking the feral but also Olaf as he scampered out of the way.

The bear turned for Katie, and Seamus tore into him. They both went down, Seamus at last getting his teeth in the bear's throat. He clamped down, and ripped.

The feral bear roared his pain and slammed himself down, flailing until he dislodged Seamus. Seamus, the bear's blood foul in his mouth, rolled in the small space, smacking into pieces of the broken bed.

Bree was up, holding on to Katie, standing against Cherie for protection. Cherie's Collar was sparking hard, as was Sean's as he ran in, though Sean's didn't slow him down. He leapt over Seamus to grab the bear and haul him back.

Seamus, gaining his feet, joined him. As he did, Tiger barreled into the room, planted his paws on the bear's back and dragged him to the floor.

The bear fought a while longer, weaker now, then collapsed and lay still, panting. The two lions were bloody, and blood gushed from the bear's thick neck and throat where Seamus had got him. Tiger kept his immense paws on the bear, holding him in place.

Walker was inside now, sighting over the barrel of a rifle. "Tranq," he said. "Get out of the way."

Before Seamus or Tiger could move, the feral beneath them shifted to human.

Sean got off him and backed away. Tiger remained but sat down on his haunches, as though conceding that it was Seamus's victory. Seamus, still lion, held the man in place.

The Shifter was about Seamus's age in both human and Shifter terms. His shaggy, unwashed hair and lines on his face made him look older, as did the haunted light in his eyes. Most of what Seamus saw was craziness, a mind that had lost sanity, though a spark of the original man remained.

"My ... cub."

The voice was cracked, barely understandable. Katie moved in Bree's arms, and Bree drew a sharp breath. "He means Katie."

The bear glared up at Seamus, angry, maddened, and grief-stricken. "Mine."

Seamus slowly shifted back to human. He kept a firm hold of the man, prepared to fight again if he had to. Francesca, still wolf, took up a stance at Seamus's side, also ready.

Katie was struggling to get down. Bree, after exchanging a look with Seamus, set Katie on her feet.

The little bear closed the small distance between herself and the Shifter. She looked down at him as he lay on the floor, her mouth coming open in a little growl of both greeting and distress.

"My cub." The man's voice was weaker but clearer. "I found ..." He put out one scarred, broken-nailed hand and touched her head. "My ... daughter."

Katie lay down on her stomach and rested her chin on the man's shoulder. There was no way she could recognize him, Seamus thought dimly. They'd found Katie when she was only a day or two old, and she'd known no parents but Francesca and the other Shifters in Kendrick's group.

But she seemed to know, without words, without being old enough even to shift to human yet, that this Shifter was her father.

He was completely feral. He'd nearly killed Katie trying to get to her, had ripped apart the human hunters without remorse, had done his best to kill Seamus. Saving him, if they could, would be tricky.

Some sanity flickered in the bear's eyes. He caught Seamus's hand. "Take care of her. Promise me."

Seamus nodded, clasping the hand that was scarred and bloody. "Like she was our own."

"Thank ..."

Then reason in his eyes died, and the red glare returned. The man snarled, the bear coming back.

Katie scampered away in alarm and hid behind Cherie's grizzly bear legs. A white streak buzzed behind Seamus, Olaf rushing to join the bears and Bree. Not from fear, Seamus sensed in amazement. Olaf had flung himself in front of them, the little polar bear ready to protect the females.

"Sean!" Seamus called.

Sean was there at once, in human form, the huge sword of the Guardian in his hands. The feral struck out at Seamus, his hands bear claws, then he fell back, spent, blood gushing from his torn throat.

Sean raised the sword high and brought it down, straight into the bear's heart.

The feral cried out, a keening that shattered the air. Then the bear shuddered once, whispered, "Thank you," let out a little sigh, and died.

His body shimmered like dust motes in sunshine, and then with a hiss, he disintegrated to nothing. A breath of wind stirred the dust and ashes, and all was silence.

Katie came out from under Cherie, sat down on her haunches, and howled. Her nose lifted to the sky, her grief clawing at Seamus's heart.

Francesca's howl twined with Katie's, Francesca mourning the loss of a fellow Shifter. The Shifters inside and outside of the house joined the cry, a shared sound of grief that one had been taken from them too soon.

Sean bent his head over the sword, his chest moving with his distressed breath. Seamus flowed back into his lion, and roared.

Seamus absorbed the grief of them all—Katie, Francesca, Sean, all the Shifters—pouring it back out in his own voice, feeling himself breaking apart.

A warmth stole through the terrible pain, the feeling of arms around him. Bree had come to his side and wrapped herself around his lion's body, burying her face in his mane.

The touch of a mate. The weight of her against him, her nearness, soothed the pain, grief, and madness. Anything feral in Seamus flowed away and was gone.

Seamus shifted back to his human form, closed Bree into his arms, and held on tight.

***

No one knew the bear's name, where he came from, or what his clan was. The next morning, Bree saw the compassion of the Shifters as they gave this crazed, unnamed, wild bear a send-off to the Goddess.

All of Shiftertown gathered in the green behind the Morrisseys' bungalow, forming concentric circles around the brazier in the middle. Seamus held Katie while Francesca placed the wooden box that contained the bear Shifter's ashes onto the flames.

"God and Goddess, receive thy child," Liam Morrissey said, his voice hushed, his face sober.

Another collective howl went up, this one more subdued than had been the cries of grief last night. The feral bear had fought for his cub and fought well. Now he deserved his rest.

Seamus walked back to Ronan's house with Bree, the two of them hand in hand. Bree had borrowed clothes from Carly this morning, a gray top and pencil-thin black pants that Carly couldn't wear at the moment. Bree's Shifter-groupie look was gone.

Seamus had set Katie down to walk on her own. She was accompanied by her now-faithful Olaf, as his polar bear cub. Francesca was never more than a step away from them, and Rebecca and Walker kept near as well. Katie would be well cared for here, Bree concluded.

Seamus was much more at ease with himself today than Bree had seen him be so far. Last night after the cleanup from the fight, she and Seamus had fallen back into bed, touching, kissing, and drifting into hard slumber.

They'd woken curled around each other, aware and wanting, but Ronan had banged on the door and told them the ritual to send the bear to the Goddess would start immediately.

No time to talk, to kiss very much, or to make wild love as Bree wanted to.

And who knew if they'd ever have time? Now that the threat to Katie was gone, what would Seamus do? Would Bree have any part of his decision? His life?

Or would she go back to being new girl in town, trying to find a job at a mechanics shop where they might let her do more than just the paperwork and making the coffee? Trying to take care of her mom, grieve for her brother, and forget she'd ever met the hot-bodied man with lion eyes.

Nope, forgetting Seamus was out of the question.

Seamus's hand tightened on hers as they neared Ronan's house. He knew this was journey's end as much as she did, and that decisions would have to be made.

Dylan was waiting for them in the big dining room. So was Tiger, with Carly. Tiger was human now, his eyes as golden as Seamus's. He'd pulled his chair next to Carly's and had his arm around her, as though daring anyone to try to keep them apart.

"Hey, sweetie," Carly said to Bree as she dropped into the chair Seamus pulled out for her. "You all right?"

"Tired." Bree tried not to feel empty when Seamus left her and went to Sean, who'd accompanied them here.

Rebecca, Bree's mother, and Ronan's mate, Elizabeth, came out of the kitchen with plates piled with muffins, scones, and other good things. They set them out, Nadine fussing a little, which Bree knew meant she was jonesing for a cigarette. She wouldn't smoke around the cubs or Carly, but her fingers kept twitching.

Nadine stopped to smooth Bree's hair and kiss the top of her head. "Don't worry, honey. We'll go home, and you can have a hot bath and sleep all day. At least, until the hammering starts. That Dylan said he'd send his Shifters over to fix the attic and the ceiling. Isn't that nice of him?" She plopped into the chair next to Bree. "Of course, I'll believe it when I see it. Repairmen always say they'll show up, and then you wait three days."

"I think they'll come," Bree said. Shifters kept their word.

"Well, I'm just glad Remy was there to help out. I told you he was."

Bree hid a sigh. "It was a broken water pipe, Mom." Or had it been? If so, it had broken at a very convenient moment. Bree decided it would be nice to believe, with her mother, that Remy was still watching over them. One day, she'd take Seamus up to the attic with her to investigate—ask him about his theory that the house was on a ley line with a gate to the Fae lands ... That is, if he was around for her to ask.

Nadine shrugged, reaching for a scone and tearing it open on one of the little plates Elizabeth was handing around. "You see it your way; I see it mine."

Bree decided not to argue with her. She'd let her mother be comforted by Remy's presence—real or imagined. And with the weirdness they'd experienced the last couple days ... well, who knew?

Dylan cleared his throat. He barely made a sound, and yet all conversation ceased and all eyes turned to him.

"Sean," Dylan said to his son. "What did you find out?"

"That Seamus *is* our clan," Sean said. Pride rang in his voice. "A cousin—very distant—and from Scotland, but we can forgive him for that in time." He grinned. "The Guardian network doesn't lie."

Seamus said nothing. He didn't look happy to be included in the Morrissey family, but not unhappy either. *Bewildered and in shock* was a better way of putting it, Bree decided.

"What about the bear?" Dylan asked.

"He could have been one of many, unfortunately," Sean said. "Those who didn't take the Collar and were left to themselves often went feral. But Katie's mum, she was a bear from a clan up in Manitoba, from a Shiftertown. She'd run off with this un-Collared bear, and the Shiftertown didn't know where. Poor lass obviously didn't make it in the wild, and Katie's father already must have been on his way to feral, or the mum wouldn't have died alone. Seamus found Katie ... and the rest we can guess. The father went looking for Katie, couldn't find her, since Kendrick's Shifters were so good at hiding. But he couldn't give up, no matter how long it took."

Seamus drifted from him to stand behind Bree. His warmth cushioned her, the chair moved with his strength as he rested his hands on its back.

"Not all un-Collared Shifters go feral," Seamus said in a quiet voice.

"We know that," Sean said. "I mean, we're learning that. Knowing more about you would help us a lot."

Seamus's hands tightened on the chair. "I'm not a lab rat. That's one reason we refused to come in twenty years ago—the experiments. Dissections." Francesca made a noise of agreement.

"No, no," Sean said quickly. "Shifters don't do that to other Shifters. You're family now. And Francesca and Katie, our guests. You're welcome in Shiftertown as long as you want to be here. No Collars. No needles. No drugs."

Tiger gave Sean a growl, as though reminding him, *You got that right.*

Broderick, who'd come in with Dylan, asked the question Bree wanted to. "What about Seamus thinking he was going feral? He was really worried about it. I was too, if you want to know."

"Not feral," Tiger said at once. "More like me."

"Oh, great," Broderick grimaced. "You mean he's another crazy?"

Tiger growled again, but more in a mock-threatening way, as though the two went back and forth like this all the time.

"I'm not sure," Dylan said, his blue eyes on Seamus. "I've never met one, and I might be wrong." His gaze sharpened. "I think you, son, are a Shifter empath."

Seamus went completely still. "What the hell is a Shifter empath?"

Dylan didn't look away. "You pick up the emotions of other Shifters. Use them to help the other Shifter—either by drawing it off, or at least understanding what they're going through. You weren't becoming feral. You were perfectly fine when you were in Bree and Nadine's house with us. You knew there was something wrong at your safe house in the middle of nowhere when your normal Shifter instinct said you were safe. Francesca didn't notice the problem, did she?"

Francesca shook her head. She watched Seamus, gray gaze wary but interested. "I thought Seamus was being overly cautions, though I didn't disagree with him."

"You found Katie," Dylan went on. "In the entire wilderness, you just happened to find her in time to save her life. I think you homed in on her distress."

Seamus's hold on the chair tightened even more until Bree was surprised the wood didn't splinter. "If that's true, why haven't I noticed it all this time? I think I would have at some point, don't you?"

Dylan shrugged. "Maybe it only flares when the anguish of the Shifter is great enough to pull you in. Maybe other times, it's subtle enough that you think it only natural compassion. I notice you haven't been able to stay away from Bree. You found her and you're hanging on to her."

Seamus said nothing. He bent to Bree, touching his lips to her neck, and didn't answer.

"What does all this mean?" Bree was getting a little tired of Dylan's profound announcements. "That you're going to make Seamus stay here while you watch him and see what he can do? He spent all this time successfully *not* being trapped, and now you want him to lock himself in with you so you can study this empathic ability? Or are you going to let him go? I think you need to answer, Mr. Dylan Morrissey. Right now."

Chapter Sixteen

Seamus felt Bree's anxiousness and anger. *Felt* it, for real, coming up into him. He also felt her desire, both physical and emotional. For him.

Empathy? Or a Shifter knowing his true mate?

"My daughter asked you a good question," Nadine said, plucking another scone to pieces. "Well? What's it going to be?"

Sean and Dylan looked only at Seamus, no one else. "We discussed it," Sean said slowly. "Me and Dad and Liam. And we decided ..." He let out his breath. "That we'd be sorry excuses for Shifters if we made Seamus stay. You're free to go, lad. Anywhere you wish. We'd like to hang on to Katie, but only for her own protection until she's of an age to decide for herself, but you ... " Sean lifted his hands. "It's whatever you want. Francesca, you too."

Now everyone was staring at Seamus. The many pairs of eyes on him—the intense blue ones of the Morrisseys, dark ones of Ronan and Rebecca, the light blue of Walker, interested ones of Carly and Bree's mother, gray of Broderick and also of Francesca—made Seamus a little cagey. They were waiting to see what he'd do. Accept? Or run?

Francesca said, after drawing a breath, "I'm staying with Katie."

Seamus figured she would. Katie was hers now.

The only person who didn't look at him was Bree. Seamus didn't want to have the conversation he needed with her in front of all those stares, so he lifted her to her feet and stilled her startled questions by pulling her out of the room.

None of the others followed or called after them. They knew.

Seamus took Bree up the stairs to the room they were sharing. Behind them, he heard the Shifters and their human mates burst out talking at once, the crowd making enough noise to drown out an army. All the better.

Seamus led Bree into the bedroom and closed the door. She faced him in the middle of the floor, her lake-blue eyes enormous.

"What are you going to do?" Bree asked him.

Seamus stripped off his shirt. "Right now? Make love to you like I can't stop. Like I've wanted to since I met you. Like I would have if we hadn't kept getting interrupted."

He growled the last words as he kicked out of his jeans. He'd put on underwear today in deference to the ceremony, and that came off too.

Bree didn't snap her gaze away, or scream, or try to run. She looked him up and down. "Nice."

"Glad you like it. Join me if you want. Your choice. I would never force you." Seamus took a step toward her, tenderness sweeping through him along with need. "I would never hurt you." He brushed Bree's hair from her face, reveling in the silken touch of her hair, her skin. "Never."

Bree ran her fingers up his chest to the hollow of his throat. "And after?" She studied his collarbone, not meeting his eyes. "Are you going to disappear forever?"

"I haven't decided." Seamus's heartbeat sped, the warmth in him becoming surging heat. "Whatever I decide, I want it to be with you. I can't offer you a damn thing—life in a bedroom in Shiftertown, or hiding out in a safe house ... somewhere. It would suck."

"That all depends. I really liked that bungalow you found downtown. It's cute. Or will be after we fix it up." A sparkle lit Bree's eyes, then dimmed. "What I don't want is for you to be caught because you stuck around to be with me. I don't want to watch you be rounded up, or whatever it's called, arrested because you don't have a Collar, forced to wear one, or killed." She pushed against his chest and stepped away. "I won't be the cause of that. I'd rather know you were out there—free—even if it means you can't be with me."

Tears beaded on her eyelashes, and Bree closed her mouth, as though fearing to say too much.

Seamus put his hands on her shoulders and drew her to him again. *Not enough.* He put his arms all the way around her, sinking into her warmth, kissing the curve of her neck.

"I know what freedom is now." Seamus kissed Bree's throat and then lifted his head to look into her eyes. "True freedom is being with the one you love, no matter what. It's not a place or a time, or running through fields looking for somewhere to hide." He brushed a kiss to her mouth. "It's loving who you need to love."

Bree's lips parted. "Are you saying you love me, Seamus McGuire? After knowing me two days? Most of those on the run?"

Seamus gave her a shrug. "It can happen fast. When it's right, it shouts to you. I'm an empath; you know I'm right."

Bree put her hands on her hips. "Is that going to make you full of yourself? Because we'll have to work on that."

"Maybe. None of that matters, though, until *you* answer. Do you want to be with me, love?"

Bree lost her cocky smile. She rose on tiptoes and held him, her tears wetting his cheek. "Crap on a crutch, Seamus. Of course I want to be with you. Always. To hell with us only knowing each other two days—who gets to set the time-limit rule? I love *you*. I know this better than anything."

"Good." Seamus let out the breath he'd been holding, the dizziness of it smacking him. He started to fall and swung them both around so they landed on the bed, Seamus on top of Bree. He pressed her wrists into the mattress, and she smiled up at him. "Because I've decided to stay in Shiftertown. I don't want to leave Katie, and Sean's right. I can help them."

Sean had told him today about a few things they were working on with the Collars, trying to get them removed from all Shifters. Going feral was a danger, and Seamus's ability to survive without one could make a difference.

"But I'm only staying if you'll come visit me," Seamus said. "And do this ..."

He kissed her. Bree wrapped herself around him, opening to him, deepening the kiss. The fabric of her pants brushed his skin and lit every fire inside him.

"I'll do more than visit," Bree said when the kiss ended. "I'll shack up with you. I'm a Shifter groupie, remember? Or at least, I used to be. That's what we groupies dream of doing, you know, moving in with a Shifter. Now that I've got a Shifter of my own, though, I won't need to dress up and hang out anymore."

"I don't know." Seamus traced around her eyes where the cat makeup had been. "Maybe you can wear the makeup and costume sometimes. The cat's ears are damn sexy."

"Ooh, kinky, are you? This sounds like fun."

Seamus drew his fingers down her white blouse, aching for her. "You're wearing too many clothes right now."

"They're Carly's. Cute, aren't they? She has good taste."

"You'll have to buy her more," Seamus growled.

Shifters could rip into clothes swiftly and precisely. In the work of a few moments, the shirt and pants and her underwear lay in shreds around them, Bree squealing in delighted surprise.

Her cries softened to those of pleasure, and then a groan as Seamus slid inside her.

The bed creaked as Bree drew her hands down his back. Seamus forgot about pain, sorrow, grief, hurt, emptiness, and filled himself with Bree. Her generous love, her smiles, her beauty, her sensual little growl as he started to move.

Seamus was one with his mate, feeling her joy, her love surrounding him and making him whole. Everything he needed.

End

Please continue for a preview of

White Tiger

Book 8
of the

Shifters Unbound series

by

Jennifer Ashley

White Tiger

Chapter One

It was almost time. Addison Price slid the coffeepot back on the heater, unable to keep her eye from the clock. The diner closed at midnight. Every night at eleven fifty-five on the dot, he came in.

Tonight, though, eleven fifty-five came and went. And eleven fifty-six, fifty-seven.

She'd have to close up. The owner liked everything shut down right at midnight. He'd come in about fifteen minutes later and start going through the accounts for the day.

Eleven fifty-eight. The last customer, a farmer in a John Deere cap he must have picked up forty years ago from all the grime on it, grinned at her and said, "Night, Addie. Time to go home to the wife."

He said that every night. Addie only smiled at him and waved good-bye.

Eleven fifty-nine. In one minute, she'd have to lock the door, turn the Open sign around to Closed, help with the clean up, and then go home. Her sister and three kids would be asleep, school day tomorrow. Addie would creep in as usual, take a soothing shower, play on the Internet a little to unwind, and then fall asleep. Her unwavering routine.

Tonight, though, she wouldn't be able to analyze every single thing the white-and-black-haired man said to her and decide whether he liked her or was just making conversation.

The second hand on the analog clock above the pass to the kitchen swept down from the twelve toward the six. Eleven-fifty nine and thirty seconds. Forty. Forty-five.

Addie sighed and moved to the glass front door.

Which opened as she approached it, bringing in warmth of a Texas night, and the man.

Addie quickly changed reaching for the door's lock to yanking the door open wide and giving him her sunniest smile. "Hello, there. Y'all come on in. You made it just in time."

The big man gave her his polite nod and walked past her with an even stride, the black denim coat he always wore brushing jeans that hugged the most gorgeous butt Addie had seen in all her days. Because this diner's clientele had plenty of farmers, utility workers, and bikers just passing through, she'd seen her fair share of not-so-good backsides in jeans ... or slipping inappropriately above waistbands.

Her man was different. His behind was worth a second, third, and fourth look. He was tall but not lanky, his build that of a linebacker in fine training, his shoulders and chest stretching his black T-shirt. The footwear under the blue jeans was always either gray cowboy boots or black motorcycle boots.

Tonight, it was the motorcycle boots, supple leather hugging his ankles.

And, as always, Addie's man carried the sword. He kept it wrapped in dark cloth, a long bundle he held in his hand and tucked beside his seat when he sat down and ordered. At first Addie had thought the bundle held a gun—a rifle or shotgun—and she'd had to tell him that the owner, Bo, didn't allow firearms of any kind in his diner. She'd lock it up for him if he wanted while he ate. They had a special locker for the hunters who were regulars.

The man had shot her a quizzical look from his incredibly sexy green eyes, pulled back the cloth, and revealed the hilt of a sword.

A sword, for crap's sake. A big one, with a silver hilt. Addie had swallowed hard and said that maybe it was okay if he kept it down beside his chair. He'd given her a curt nod and covered the hilt back up.

But that was just him. He was like no man Addie had ever met in her life. His eyes were an incredible green she couldn't look away from once he caught her with a gaze. The eyes went with his hard face, which had been knocked around in his life, but he still managed to be handsome enough to turn the head of whatever woman happened to be in this late. Which, most nights, was only Addie.

His hair, though, was the weirdest thing. It was white, like a Scandinavian white-blond, but striped with black. As though he'd gone in for a dye job one day and left it half finished. Or maybe he simply liked the look.

Except, Addie would swear it was natural. Dyes left an unusual sheen or looked brittle after a while. His hair glistened under the lights, each strand soft, weaving with the others in a short cut that suited his face. Addie often studied his head as he bent over his pie, and she'd clutch her apron to keep from reaching out and running her fingers through his interesting hair.

In sum — this man was hotter than a Texas wind on a dry summer day. Addie could feel the sultry heat when she was around him. At least, she sure started to sweat whenever she looked at him.

For the last month or so, he'd come in every night near to closing time, order the last pieces of banana cream pie and the apple pie with streusel and eat while Addie locked the door and went through her rituals for the night. When Bo arrived through the back door, the man would go out the front, taking his sword ... and the other things he always brought.

They came in now, walking behind him — three little boys, the oldest one following the two younger ones. The oldest one's name was Robbie, and he brought up the rear, looking around as though guarding his two little brothers with his life.

"Hello, Robbie," Addie said. "Brett, Zane. How are you tonight?"

The two littlest would chorus *Fine*, but Robbie only gave her a polite nod, mimicking his father. If he was Robbie's father. The youngest ones had the man's green eyes and white-and-black hair, but Robbie didn't look like any of them. He had dark brown hair and eyes that were gray — a striking-looking kid, but Addie figured he wasn't related to the others. Adopted maybe, or a nephew. Whatever, the guy looked after all three with protective fierceness, not letting anyone near them.

They took four stools at the counter, as usual. Robbie sat on the seat farthest from the door, Zane and Brett perched in the next two seats, with their dad next to them, his bulk between them and whoever might enter the diner. These seats were also not in front of the diner's windows, but at the very end of the counter, almost in the hall to the bathrooms.

Addie took up the coffeepot and poured a cup of fully caffeinated brew for black-and-white guy and three ice waters for the boys. She'd offered them cokes when they first came in, but their dad didn't like them having sugared drinks.

Considering how much pie they put away, Addie didn't blame him. Sweet sodas on top of that would have them wired to the gills all night.

"You almost missed the pie," Addie said to the boys as she set the dripping glasses of water on the counter. "We had a run on it today. But I saved you back a few pieces in the fridge." She winked at them. "I'll just run and get them. That's three banana creams and an apple streusel, right?"

She looked into the father's green eyes, and stopped.

She'd never seen him look at her like that. There was a hunger in his gaze, powerful and intense. He skewered her with it, and Addie looked back at him, her mouth open, her heart constricting before it started pounding.

Men had looked at her with suggestion before, but they'd always accompanied it with a half-amused smile as though laughing at themselves or telling Addie she'd have a great time if she conceded.

This was different. Black-and-white man studied her with a wanting that was palpable, as though any second he'd climb over the counter and come at her.

After a second, he blinked, and the look was gone. He hadn't intended her to catch him.

The blink showed Addie something else. Behind the interest, his eyes held great distraction and deep worry.

Something had happened tonight, some reason he'd come here going on five minutes late.

Addie knew better than to ask him if everything was all right. He wouldn't answer. The man was not one for casual conversation. The boys talked, but kept their answers general. They had not betrayed with one word where they were from, where they went to school, what they liked to do for fun, or why their dad kept them up this late every night.

Addie simply gave them all her smile, said, "I'll be right back," and ducked into the kitchen to fetch the pie she'd held back for them.

She took out pieces, already sliced on their plates, and sprinkled a little extra cocoa powder on the banana cream ones from the dented shaker on the shelf.

The guy who washed dishes — Bo went through a new one about every two weeks — wasn't there. He liked to ducked out for a smoke right at closing time, coming back in when Bo got there to finish the cleanup. Addie hummed, alone in the kitchen, her pulse still high from that look black-and-white man had given her.

If Addie marched out there and said to him, sure, she was interested — in a discreet way in front of his kids — would he break down and tell her his name?

Or would he take her somewhere and make love to her with silent strength, the same way he walked and ate? Would Addie mind that?

She pictured him above her in the dark, his green eyes on her while she ran her hands all over his tight, beautiful body.

Nope, she wouldn't mind that at all.

She picked up two pieces of pie, still humming. At the same time, she heard a scratching at the back door.

Bo? Addie set down the pie and walked over. Bo always used his key to get in — they kept the back door locked. Even in this small town that was pretty safe, robbers passing through might seize an opportunity.

Bo often couldn't get his key into the lock — his hands shook with a palsy that ran in his family. The dishwasher often had to help him, or Addie would open the door for him.

Bo was a bit early, but he was sometimes. Addie reached for the door, just as something banged into it.

"Bo? You okay?" Addie unlocked the deadbolt, carefully pulled the door open, and peeked out.

The door fell inward, a heavy weight on it. Addie looked down.

A curious detachment came over her as she saw the dishwasher, a guy of about thirty with greasy brown hair and beard stubble. He was dead, his brown eyes staring sightlessly. She knew he was dead because he had a gaping red hole where his heart used to be.

If this had been a movie, Addie would be screaming, fainting, sobbing, saying *Oh, my God,* or running outside crying, *Somebody, help!*

Instead, she stood there, as though caught in treacle, unable to move, think, talk, or even breathe.

A faint noise sounded outside, and Addie raised her head. She saw the round muzzle of a gun, one of the automatic ones that shot however many rounds a minute. Her breath poured back into her lungs, burning, and she knew she was looking at her own death.

A rush of air passed her, and the door slammed closed. At the same time a pair of strong arms closed around her, propelling her to the floor, the man with black-and-white hair landing on top of her.

In the front of the diner, every window shattered as bullets fired through it. Glass flew through the open pass between kitchen and dining area, as did bullets, shards of cups and plates, tatters of napkins.

The kids, Addie thought in panic. *Where were the boys?*

There they were, huddled against the door to the freezer. How the man had gotten them in here so fast and out of sight and then come for Addie. she didn't know, but her body went limp with relief to see them.

"Who's doing this?" Addie squeaked. "What—"

The man clamped his hand over her mouth. "Shh," he said, his voice a low rumble. "I need to you to be very quiet, all right?"

End of Excerpt

Please continue for a preview of

Bad Wolf

Book 7.5
of the

Shifters Unbound series

by

Jennifer Ashley

Bad Wolf

Chapter One

Broderick McNaughton woke with a raging headache, dry mouth, and what felt like hot bands around his wrists. *What the fuck?*

He didn't remember getting this drunk. He remembered hanging out at Liam's bar for a while then heading to the fight club with Spike. Spike was a refreshing guy to be with—he didn't talk a lot, wasn't noticeably crazy, and didn't expect you to speak if there was nothing important to say.

Spike could also kick ass in the fight ring and go out for pizza. Broderick had joined him for the pizza tonight—anything to keep from heading home to his three pain-in-the-ass younger brothers, a half-feral Shifter Feline, and the half-feral's very protective human mate.

After he'd said good night to Spike, Broderick had dropped in on Sean Morrissey, the Shiftertown's Guardian, to report on ongoing tracker business. He'd sat with Sean on his back porch a while, watching Sean cuddle his sleeping cub on his lap.

Somewhere between saying good night to Sean and heading home across the dark common yards behind Shifter houses, Broderick had lost consciousness.

The bands around his wrists were real — heavy-duty metal handcuffs. Strong enough for a Shifter, tight enough that even if he shifted to wolf, he wouldn't be able to slip his big paws out.

Broderick couldn't see and could barely breathe, because there was a bag over his head, its drawstring tight around his throat.

What the holy fuck?

Broderick's first instinct was to struggle, to break out of his restraints no matter how strong and kill whoever had done this. His second instinct told him to shut up and lie still and figure out where he was. No sense busting out of the cuffs and bag to find five guys with machine guns waiting for him. Cunning was sometimes the better part of valor.

Broderick remained motionless. He might not be able to see, but he could hear and he could scent, which for a Shifter, were more important senses at times like these.

He smelled humans, not in the room with him, but definitely nearby. His hackles rose. He doubted these humans were police or Shifter Bureau's mighty patrollers — *they'd* have put him into a sterilized cage, not bothering with the head bag. When he woke, a Shifter Bureau worker with a clipboard would explain why they'd decided to round him up, cage him, and terminate him.

So, if he hadn't been caught by Shifter Bureau or police, that left Shifter hunters.

Shifter hunters were humans who boasted of stalking un-Collared, rogue Shifters to bring them in or kill them. They weren't allowed to hunt Shifters with Collars, like Broderick, but because un-Collared Shifters weren't thick on the ground, the hunters often bent the rules. They'd go after anything Shifter, pretending not to notice that the Shifter they killed actually had a black and silver Collar around his neck. They'd apologize profusely, but said Shifter would already be dead.

Even as these thoughts formed, Broderick had his doubts. Hunters would have also stuck him into a cage or simply shot him. Besides, no way human hunters could have sneaked into Shiftertown. It was too well guarded by Shiftertown's trackers, of which Broderick was one.

Then who?

He felt cold stone under his body, smelled musty, dank air behind the head bag. Floorboards creaked, but overhead. He also smelled damp lint and laundry detergent, which meant a washing machine and dryer nearby. Conclusion—he was in somebody's basement.

Humans lived in this house, not Shifters. So again—*what the fuck?*

He smelled another odor, one of warm plastic, and he heard a hum of electronics. Interesting.

Broderick should have said *screw it* tonight and tried to see Joanne. He could be curled up on the sofa with her, watching TV, or ignoring the TV while they explored kissing and touching. Instead he'd been noble and left her alone. What was wrong with him?

A door scraped open, and footsteps headed down a flight of wooden stairs. Heavy treads, men, and the lighter tread of a female. The light steps moved swiftly past the heavy.

"Is this him?" the woman asked, breathless, eager.

Goddess, please don't tell me this is a Shifter groupie who wants a shag. I might throw up on her.

The bag loosened, and then was ripped from Broderick's head. He still couldn't see—a blindfold covered his eyes. Light penetrated the cloth, a very bright one, as though someone shone a flashlight on his face.

He felt breath touch his cheek, feminine, almost sweet, but cold and rapid with excitement. A small hand in his hair raised his head. Broderick suppressed his growl, his urge to snap out of the restraints and attack.

"Are you sure this is him?" the woman asked. She sounded young, especially for a human, past teen years, but not much. Broderick's head was moved left and right, the woman's breath coming faster. "Wait ..." She released him abruptly, and Broderick's head clunked to the cement floor.

"What the hell did you bring me?" she demanded.

"The Shifter who came out of the Guardian's back door," a man answered. His voice was deep, holding strength, yet Broderick heard and smelled his fear. Of a woman not much older than a cub?

"This isn't him!" She climbed to her feet, her voice shrill. The flashlight beamed against Broderick's blindfold. "Does this *look* like a Feline? He's Lupine, you idiot."

"How the hell are we supposed to tell the difference?" the man asked with the annoyance of a scared person. "You didn't give us a picture to go by."

"Four Shifters live in that house," the young woman snapped. "Two are female. I would have thought you had at least a fifty-fifty chance of snatching the right *male*. But no, you had to bring me someone completely off the chart. He's obviously a grunt worker. No use to me at all!"

Was she insane? The two Shifters who lived in Sean's house were Sean, the Shiftertown Guardian, and his father, Dylan. If this woman's thugs had captured Dylan, he'd have killed her by now and all these guys too—and joined Spike for *three* pizzas. Sean wouldn't have been much safer for her, but maybe a little more polite before he left their bodies in broken piles.

Ah, the lucky sons of bitches. They'd snagged *Broderick* instead. He'd just bounce them around for fun and then call people to pick them up and charge them with hunting a Collared Shifter. Handy to know a guy in Shifter Bureau, one who wasn't a total dickhead.

"Get out!" the woman yelled at the men. "You useless shits; get the hell out!"

"You owe us." The tremor in the man's voice betrayed his fear, but he spoke with the determination of one who would do anything for money. "It wasn't easy to bring him here. Maybe he can help you anyway."

"Seriously?" the young woman cried. "I gave you half up front. The deal was the other half on delivery, but you didn't deliver, did you? If you come back with the right one, *maybe* I'll pay you. Or you can just get the hell out before I kill you."

Broderick heard a click of metal, the sound of a gun cocking.

"Whoa," the man said. "You are one crazy bitch. We're out of here."

He was walking even as he spoke. Footsteps sounded on the stairs, moving swiftly, then a door slammed. The floorboards creaked overhead, and then another above banged.

Broderick was left alone in the basement with an insane woman who had a gun. *Great.*

A slim hand hooked around the blindfold and tore it away. Broderick blinked at the sudden glare of the flashlight, his mouth dry as linen.

When the light moved he could see the sharp-boned face of a young woman with short, unnaturally black hair. Her skin was fair and freckled, her mouth black with lipstick. The nails of the hand around the pistol had been painted black to match.

"No offense, Shifter," she said, her voice clear and youthful. She couldn't be more than twenty-something, the same age as Cherie, a young grizzly Shifter who lived not far from Broderick. "But I can't let you tell them about me."

Broderick could argue. He could say that a Shifter missing from Shiftertown would be a big deal, because they were all watched pretty closely. Joanne would worry when she couldn't reach Broderick, then she'd get his aunt worried, and then Aunt Cora would send his brothers to track him. When they started panicking, they'd go to Liam, who would organize a search. Tiger would get involved, and there was nowhere in the world this woman could hide from the messed-up shit that was Tiger.

But Broderick figured that argument would be a waste of breath. He wasn't good at arguing anyway.

He summoned all his Shifter strength, balled his fists, slammed his wrists apart, and rolled into the young woman's legs at the same time.

The cuffs remained whole, made to withstand Shifters, but Broderick's rolling bulk knocked the young woman off balance, and she went down.

Broderick kept moving. They hadn't bound his ankles, and he got his feet under him, one heavy boot kicking the gun out of the young woman's hand. The gun went off as her finger was tugged from the trigger, a bullet thudding into the wooden ceiling

She shouted vile words at him and scrambled to reach the gun. Broderick snarled in pain as he yanked at the cuffs again, calling on his strength to jerk free of them. He managed to break the chain between them, and now he had a matching pair of metal bracelets around his wrists.

Good enough. He'd done a quick assessment of the basement as soon as he could see and had already chosen his path of escape.

The long room had a washer and dryer standing on a cement platform on one end. Above these, at the top of the wall, were narrow windows leading outside. The rest of the room held tables upon tables of blinking computers, explaining the scent of warming plastic and the sound of working electronics.

Stacked CPU boxes flickered with lights, several monitors were pushed side-by-side, a few laptops were open, screens swirling with patterns, and keyboards lay here and there. The floor under the table was littered with junk—strands of wires, metal and plastic pieces, and small solid black boxes—a lot of stuff Broderick couldn't identify.

He took all this in between one heartbeat and the next, then he was across the room, on top of the washing machine, shifting to his between-beast, pulling the window out of its slot. He smashed glass and frame to the floor and the yard outside. The woman screamed.

She'd reached the gun. She fired two rounds as Broderick shifted completely to wolf and leapt for open air. His clothes finished shredding and falling away, and a sudden pain in his leg made him yelp.

The cuffs still clung to Broderick's wolf paws—the woman had judged the size and strength of them well. But he could squash himself flat if he needed to, and he did to scramble through the window, his most direct route of escape.

Pain burned in Broderick's leg as he scrambled out, but he made it. It was pitch dark, and Broderick had no idea where he was. Behind him, the woman was still screaming, still shooting, but the bullets pinged harmlessly inside the basement.

He stood up, panting. There were large houses nearby, but no lights shone in them, and they had the air of being empty, abandoned. Beyond them lay open fields of nothing. The young woman wasn't worried about anyone hearing her shooting, which meant these houses were a long way from anywhere.

Broderick didn't linger. He took off across the dirt and dried grass of the field on his swift wolf legs, scrambling over rocks and brush, putting as much distance between himself and the houses as he could.

Now to figure out where the hell he was and how he was going to get back to Shiftertown, alone, a wolf, with no clothes and no money.

And still this is better than being at home with that crazy-ass half-feral Shifter, Broderick thought as he limped on. *Damn, my life truly sucks.*

End of Excerpt

About the Author

New York Times bestselling and award-winning author Jennifer Ashley has written more than 75 published novels and novellas in romance, urban fantasy, and mystery under the names Jennifer Ashley, Allyson James, and Ashley Gardner. Her books have been nominated for and won Romance Writers of America's RITA (given for the best romance novels and novellas of the year), several *RT BookReviews* Reviewers Choice awards (including Best Urban Fantasy, Best Historical Mystery, and Career Achievement in Historical Romance), and Prism awards for her paranormal romances. Jennifer's books have been translated into more than a dozen languages and have earned starred reviews in *Booklist*. When Jennifer isn't writing, she enjoys cooking, hiking, playing flute and guitar, and building dollhouses and dollhouse miniatures.

More about Jennifer's books and series can be found at www.jenniferashley.com

Made in the USA
Middletown, DE
23 August 2015